"Did I misread what I saw? Was it all in my imagination?"

Lie to her. That was all he needed to do. One tiny lie, let her down easy, and this crisis was averted. Moments passed. It was his tactical advantage and he knew he should take it.

But looking into her precious brown eyes, her sweet face, he couldn't do it. "No. You didn't imagine it."

She took a step closer. He took a step back.

"Why, Derek?" Her question was barely more than a whisper. "Why have you stayed away from me all this time? You've had to know I wanted to be with you."

"Molly, our worlds don't mix. I'm not the right person for you."

"Don't you think I should get to be the judge of that?"

SPECIAL FORCES SAVIOR

JANIE CROUCH

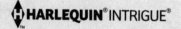

HARLEQUIN® INTRIGUE®

To my grandparents: Mittie and Quinton King, as you celebrate your
70th(!!!) wedding anniversary this very month. All the romantic stories
I'll ever write will never compare to the true love you've lived in a
lifetime together. You've taught me that marriage is 80% adoration and
20% exasperation, but no matter what, it is always filled with respect.
Thank you for being a living example of what love is to your children,
your grandchildren and your great-grandchildren.
Your legacy is many things, but most important, it is love.

ISBN-13: 978-0-373-69880-6

Special Forces Savior

Copyright © 2016 by Janie Crouch

Recycling programs
for this product may
not exist in your area.

www.Harlequin.com

Janie Crouch has loved to read romance her whole life. She cut her teeth on Harlequin Romance novels as a preteen, then moved on to a passion for romantic suspense as an adult. Janie lives with her husband and four children overseas. Janie enjoys traveling, long-distance running, movie-watching, knitting and adventure/obstacle racing. You can find out more about her at janiecrouch.com.

Books by Janie Crouch

Omega Sector: Critical Response

Special Forces Savior

Omega Sector

Infiltration
Countermeasures
Untraceable
Leverage

Harlequin Intrigue

Primal Instinct

Visit the Author Profile page at
Harlequin.com for more titles.

CAST OF CHARACTERS

Derek Waterman—Tactical Teams Specialist for the Omega Sector: Critical Response Division. Raised on a ranch in Wyoming, and with a past in Special Forces, he's a warrior at heart and a loner. He's on the trail of terrorists who bombed Chicago two weeks ago.

Molly Humphries—Criminal pathologist and head of the forensic lab at Omega Sector. She is brilliant, focused and logical, except when it comes to Derek Waterman.

Jon Hatton—Behavior analyst and pilot for the Critical Response Division. Working the Chicago bombing case with Derek.

Liam Goetz—Part of the Hostage Rescue Unit of Omega Sector. Friends with Derek and Jon and helping them with the case.

Steve Drackett—Director of Omega Sector: Critical Response.

James Donald Hougland—US congressman on the oversight committee for the Chicago bombing.

Robert Edmundson—US senator and chair of the oversight committee.

Pablo Belisario—Colombian drug lord.

Andrea Gordon—Profiler for the Critical Response Division.

Brandon Han—Brilliant Critical Response Division agent. Licensed to practice law.

Chapter One

Pinned down behind his car with someone shooting at him from across the street was not how Omega Sector agent Derek Waterman had planned to spend his afternoon. He wasn't exactly sure how he had planned to spend his afternoon, but this was definitely not it.

Derek slid closer to the ground as a bullet whizzed past his head and shattered the concrete behind him.

Whoa. Too close.

The saving grace in this situation was at least the entire block was empty of any innocent bystanders. No upstanding citizen had much reason to be in this section of West Philly. The less upstanding citizens had exited when Derek and his team had shown up, obviously law enforcement, and the shooting had started.

"Uh, what exactly was the intel you got on this place again, Derek?" Jon Hatton asked from where he was also pinned down a few feet away. Although highly trained in weapons and combat as all Omega Sector's Critical Response agents were, Jon was primarily a behavior analyst in the Crisis Management Unit.

"What's the matter? You having problems remembering how to use your weapon, Jon? Too much analyzing, not enough action in your life?" Liam Goetz, the other team member, smacked his gum and grinned. As a member of

Omega's Hostage Rescue team, no one ever asked Liam if he remembered how to use a weapon. Liam had pretty much been born with one in his hand.

"I'm just asking to see if there is any sort of plan here besides hide behind the car until the bad guys run out of ammo," Jon responded. "Which, at the rate they're shooting, should be sometime next week."

True, the number of shots being fired at them seemed to be dwindling. The people in the building obviously weren't trying to kill Derek and his team, just keep them pinned. But damned if this entire situation wasn't starting to piss Derek off.

The empty apartment building across the street gave the enemy the tactical advantage. That advantage wasn't something Derek, as the lead tactical team specialist of Omega's SWAT generally gave up.

But the intel they'd received on this location had required an immediate response. Time for tactical analysis hadn't been available. Thus, the taking cover behind their SUV as the bullets flew by their heads.

Derek had moved in on this location so quickly because it had been the first substantial lead pertaining to a terrorist attack on Chicago two weeks earlier. A bombing that had killed or injured over five hundred people.

None of the leads Omega had followed up on until now—and there had been hundreds of them—had provided any useful intel. Each location had been totally cold.

Another bullet flew by. This location definitely wasn't cold.

"All right, to hell with this." Derek looked over at Liam. "Jon and I will lay down cover-fire. You head around to the back of the building."

Liam was grinning like an idiot. He loved this sort of thing, danger be damned. "Now you're talking."

Derek nodded. "Remember, we need them alive, if at all possible."

"Hey, it's me!" Liam actually winked at them. "I wouldn't hurt a fly."

Derek rolled his eyes and heard Jon groan under his breath as Liam made his way down the line of abandoned cars parked on the street. Still using their SUV for as much cover as possible, Derek and Jon began firing their weapons toward the abandoned building, hoping to draw any return-fire back at them and away from Liam.

But there were no shots at all coming at them from the house.

Derek looked over at Jon. "Again."

Using the hood to brace his arm, Derek fired three shots at the house while Jon did the same from the rear of the vehicle. Still no return-fire. Out of the corner of his eye he saw Liam make it across the street at the side of the building. No shots were fired at him, either.

The bad guys weren't in the building anymore; they must be on the run. Whoever had been shooting at them just a few moments ago was Omega's best lead in Chicago's terrorist attack. They were the *only* lead. And now they were about to get away.

"Move in, but be careful," Derek said to Jon as they made their way forward, weapons still raised.

Derek was reaching for the knob of the door, Jon covering him from a cross angle when they heard a rapid burst of gunfire from the back of the building where Liam had been heading.

Both men backed out of the doorway and sprinted around the building without a word. Each of them knew that getting inside was secondary to helping Liam if he was under fire. As they rounded the building, Derek was relieved to see Liam unharmed, chasing a suspect farther down the road behind the apartment building. Derek and Jon continued running to catch up with them. Helping capture a known suspect was better than sticking around for what may or may not be in the house.

"Stay with them," Derek told Jon, then made a sharp turn. He would run down a parallel side street and try to cut off the runner. He forced more speed out of his legs.

As he made a sharp turn around the next group of buildings, Derek saw the perp slowing down with Liam only a few yards behind him, Jon just beyond that.

It was obvious Liam was going to catch the guy at any moment, and the perp knew it, too. He fired his weapon at the Omega agents behind his back in some haphazard fashion without even stopping his run, but the bullets didn't come anywhere near either of them.

Derek turned again and began running toward them.

"Stop!" he called out to the man, and saw distress wash over his face. The man stopped running altogether, sliding to an awkward stop.

"You're under arrest," Derek continued between breaths. "Place the gun on the ground and put your hands on your head."

The man turned around, frantically looking for another way out, but didn't put his gun down. All the Omega agents gripped their weapons tighter. Nobody wanted to shoot this suspect, he was too important. But they would if necessary. Especially if he turned his weapon on them rather than where it currently lay in his hand pointing at the ground.

"Put your weapon down," Derek repeated. He nodded toward the ground with his forehead, as the man turned back in his direction. "Do you understand? All we want to do is ask you some questions."

That wasn't entirely true, but Derek just wanted to get the man's gun out of his hand.

The man nodded and Derek eased his finger off the trigger just the slightest bit. But then, almost as if it was in slow motion, and before any of them could react, the guy brought his gun up to his own temple and fired. He crumpled to the ground, dead instantly.

Derek's curse was vile. Jon rushed up to the man and crouched down to take his pulse at the wrist, but Derek knew it was too late.

Their best lead—their *only* lead—had just blown his brains out rather than be taken into custody.

He looked over at Jon and Liam. "We need to call this in. Omega and local PD."

Liam already had his phone out. "On it."

"Okay, stay with the body until they get here." Derek turned back toward the house. "Jon, let's go see if there's anything in the house. Maybe we'll get lucky."

They hadn't gone more than a few steps before they smelled it. Smoke, coming from the building the potential terrorist had just vacated.

If possible, Derek's curse was even more vile. A burned house would destroy all possible evidence. The poor dead guy had probably just been a decoy to lure the Omega team away so whoever was left could start the fire.

Jon and Derek sprinted back to the house. Smoke was pouring out of the windows. If they were going to be able to salvage anything useful, they'd have to do it in a hurry. As safely as possible, Derek opened the back door, throwing a latex glove onto one hand to grab anything that might be useful for the investigation. Then he took off his jacket to use as a filter over his mouth.

Inside, everything was in flames. Whoever had been here had used some sort of accelerating agent, probably gasoline, to make the place burn more quickly. Bending low under the smoke, he and Jon made their way farther inside.

They'd been in the house less than a minute, squinting their way through the smoke and heat, when Jon pulled on Derek's shoulder, gesturing back toward the door. Jon was right. This was too dangerous. They needed answers about the terrorist attack, but it wasn't worth either of them losing their lives.

Derek saw a few pieces of some sort of computer hardware sitting broken on the floor. He crawled to them, wincing as his hand was burned picking up the more substantial pieces and placing them inside his jacket pocket. Jon was pulling on him again and Derek could feel the hairs singeing on his arms from the heat. It was time to go.

As they rushed to get out, Derek saw something just under the layer of smoke lying near the edge of the kitchen table. It looked like some sort of communication device, or maybe some sort of drive, about half the size of a cell phone. Derek pushed Jon toward the door, then dropped to his hands and knees to crawl to it. The smoke was now too heavy to remain upright. Derek smelled the putrid stench of burning flesh just before he felt pain on his shoulders and back. He was too close to the heat and it was burning his skin. He grabbed the device and wrapped it in his jacket, then began crawling for the door.

Or at least he hoped he was crawling in the direction of the door. He could no longer see in the smoke. Breathing was becoming damn near impossible. Derek kept crawling forward.

Hands reached from in front of him, grabbed him under the armpits and dragged him out of the building and into blessed clean and cool air.

"You are one stubborn son of a bitch," Jon murmured to him as he dragged Derek down the three steps onto the ground.

"I'm okay," Derek wheezed out, crawling a few more

steps before sprawling on the ground. The pain in his back and shoulders was uncomfortable, but not excruciating. His lungs, though, felt seared. Both men lay, watching the building burn for long minutes, Derek's lungs finally feeling a bit of ease as he continued to breathe clean air. Eventually he could hear the sirens signaling the firefighters' arrival.

"I hope you got something in there," Jon told him, obviously hearing the sirens, too. "Because the only thing that destroys evidence quicker than fire—"

"Is extinguishing it," Derek finished for him. Water, foam, the firemen themselves. All were hell on evidence.

"Yep."

"I think I might have gotten something important." Still lying in the mostly dead grass of a lawn that hadn't seen proper care for decades, Derek explained about the communication device. "We need to get it back to the lab so Molly can try to recover information from it."

Jon snickered. "Uh, o-o-okay, D-Derek." The stuttering was completely for show.

Sitting up, Derek rolled his eyes. "Shut up, Jon. She's not that bad." Derek knew he shouldn't try to defend Molly Humphries, the forensic lab director. Yeah, the pretty pathologist tended to get a little tongue-tied around Derek. But the more he tried to defend her to his colleagues when they mentioned it—which was as often as damn possible—the worse everyone teased.

Jon smiled. "Hey, you know I like sweet Molly as much as anyone. But I have to admit that watching her go from the most intelligent scientist I know to a blushing, stammering schoolgirl around you is one of my favorite pastimes."

"Shut up, Jon," Derek repeated. "Just focus on the case."

Jon was wise enough not to say anything else about Molly Humphries.

Both Jon and Derek were seen by paramedics as they waited for the firefighters to finish their job. Derek was decreed as suffering from first-degree burns on his shoulders and smoke inhalation, but didn't require further medical attention. As he and Jon watched the firefighters work diligently, neither held out much hope of finding any further evidence. They would still check.

Liam joined them once local law enforcement came to pick up the body of the guy who had shot himself. Liam had taken the dead man's prints and his weapon, as well as a sample of the man's DNA. The body would be delivered to the Omega morgue later. All the items Liam had collected would go straight back to the lab.

A dead suspect, a burnt building and a few broken pieces of possible evidence. All in all a pretty terrible day. Definitely not any closer to solving the terrorist attack on Chicago. And Derek knew they were going to get chewed out again for it. Govermental-type bigwigs all the way up the food chain were demanding answers for the bombing. Derek was scheduled to provide an update to a committee via teleconference in just a few hours.

Derek wasn't looking forward to that. Especially not now, with nothing to show.

Derek's only hope now was that Molly, with all her magic in her lab, could salvage something out of this mess. Molly had saved Derek before. He prayed she could do it again.

Chapter Two

Molly Humphries caught a look at her shoes as she carried an armful of case files across the lab to her desk. How she hated her sensible shoes. They were flat, unimaginative and...well, just *sensible*. Plain and brown.

That her shoes were a symbolic reflection of her personal life was not lost on Molly.

She had no idea why the shoes were offending her so much on this particular day, when she'd been wearing them every day for over six months. They'd faithfully seen her through long weeks at the lab where she'd sometimes put in sixty or seventy hours a week. Her shoes got the job done, gave her no cause for complaints and never drew attention to themselves for the wrong reasons.

Oh man, the metaphors just kept coming, didn't they?

She should be thankful for her shoes now, for their comfort and sensibleness, since she'd already been on her feet for ten hours, and the day wasn't close to over. Molly loved her job as director of Omega Critical Response Division's main forensic lab here in Colorado Springs. Her work was challenging and fulfilling. Molly excelled at it, both as one of the leading pathologists in the country and as supervisor of the dozen people who worked daily in the lab.

Molly stopped and added another case file to the pile she was carrying. Not that they couldn't use twice as many technicians working here. That's how much material was constantly brought in for them to process. The forensic lab handled just about everything having to do with evidence: toxicology, trace reports, forensic biology, pathology, prints, DNA and even human remains for all the Critical Response Division cases. Therefore the lab was in a constant state of backup. Hiring more technicians was on Molly's to-do list, but the qualifications and security clearance required to work at Omega made the candidate pool slim.

So for right now Molly planned to continue working twelve- to fourteen-hour days to help keep the lab producing results at the speed they were needed. Like today. She'd arrived at seven o'clock this morning and was still here even though it was nearly eight in the evening. She definitely needed to cut her sensible shoes a break.

The other lab technicians had left a couple of hours ago, but being here by herself wasn't unusual or even unpleasant. Molly didn't expect her lab technicians to put in the same crazy hours she did. Often some of them were willing to stay late or come early if Molly asked, but she tried not to impose unless it was an emergency. These people had family. Molly didn't, so it was easier for her to stay. Nobody was going to miss her at home.

Molly got along well with all the people who worked in her lab. She treated them with the respect they deserved and, in turn, they worked hard. The key was direct, clear, respectful communication. Molly prided herself that she was not only good at the science part of her job, she was good at the communication aspect with her colleagues, as well.

Derek Waterman walked through the swinging double doors of the inner lab.

Well, maybe not *all* her colleagues.

Molly turned away quickly and placed the files on her desk. She put them right smack in the middle so she wouldn't accidentally knock them over. Molly had been known to do stupid things like that while in the presence of Derek.

Jon Hatton and Liam Goetz were with Derek and none of them looked too happy. Molly could smell smoke on them from across the lab, coming from *them*. Derek had been in a fire.

"Are you okay? Is everyone okay?" Molly rushed across the room, her long French-braided brown hair swinging over the shoulder of the white lab coat she always wore. These were three of the most intelligent and able-bodied men she'd ever known, but as active Omega agents they put their lives on the line daily.

"We're fine, sweet Molly," Jon said to her as she stopped a few feet away from them. "Unless you count your boy Derek here almost being trapped in a burning building as not okay."

Molly felt the air rush out of her lungs. She looked over at Derek for just a moment, needing to take in with her own eyes that he wasn't, indeed, seriously injured. His dark brown, almost-black hair had the tousled, disheveled look it always did, the five-o'clock shadow a permanent fixture on his chiseled face. He was leaning against one of the research tables, his long legs extended in front of him. She couldn't see any signs of pain based on his body language or facial expressions. Just a slight stiffness in how he held his back.

Molly knew Derek well enough to know that meant he'd been hurt.

"Did you burn your sh-shoulders?" she asked him, the words barely coming out in a whisper. Molly pressed her lips together and looked down at her shoes. She heard Liam snicker quietly before Jon nudged him.

"Yes, but I'm okay. Very minor first-degree burns on my shoulders and back," Derek responded. "No real harm."

Molly just nodded, relieved the burns weren't serious, although she could tell he had also suffered, at least to some small degree, from smoke inhalation. Derek's sexy voice was even deeper and more gravelly than usual, and although she hated the cause, Molly couldn't help but shiver slightly at the rougher sound of it.

Of course, then she felt like a fool, as she always did when Derek was around, for the way she was acting. Molly turned to a desk behind her and pretended to sort through files. She didn't blame Jon and Liam for snickering. Her behavior every time Derek entered the room was snicker-worthy.

"We've got some evidence from a lead we followed dealing with the Chicago bombing," Liam said as he began unpacking various evidence bags and laying them out on the table.

Molly walked back around to the table so she was on the far side, careful not to look at Derek in any way, not even out of the corner of her eye. It seemed as if they had about a dozen items that needed processing.

"We need a complete work up on all of it," Jon told her. "DNA, fingerprints, any possible trace evidence. Everything."

Molly picked up one of the bags containing some sort of piece of computer hardware inside. "Was this evidence from the burning building?"

"Not all of it," Derek answered her, causing Molly to study the contents of the bag more carefully so she wouldn't have to look at him. "Some of it is from what was left of a suspect before he killed himself. But the rest is from the burnt building."

"Is the body coming in here, too? Will I need to process that?" She looked at Liam and Jon as she said it.

Liam shook his head. "Yes, but not until later. Local coroner will be bringing it by. We brought prints and DNA so you could get started."

"You know, the stuff from the fire will take longer. It will have to be manually run through the system, based on layers of damage. Probably have to use a clean room." Molly put the bag back on the table. "Put it all over on the in-processing shelf. I'll try to get somebody started on it in the morning, but it might be in the afternoon."

Both Liam and Jon started talking at her immediately, voices raised, speaking all over each other. Derek, she noticed, didn't say anything. Molly held up a hand and eventually the two men stopped talking at the same time.

"Molly, this is a priority," Liam said. "It has to do with the Chicago bombing."

"I understand, Liam, but—"

"The largest terrorist attack on American soil in over five years," Jon continued. "We need the results on all of it right away."

Molly glanced quickly at Derek. He was just standing there, arms crossed over his large chest. She looked away again, not knowing what she would do if he interjected into the argument. Molly understood the men's frustration, she really did.

She looked over at the pile of files and packages of evidence on her desk. The problem was, every case was this important to *someone*. Those packages might provide clues to missing children, or someone's murder, or the identity of a serial rapist.

Everybody needed everything right away and that just wasn't possible.

"You guys," Molly looked at Jon and Liam, and even risked a glance at Derek. "I—I'm sorry. We're backed up in here."

"Molly." Liam wouldn't let it go. "We need all this now. It's vital."

Molly threw her arm out toward the files on her desk. "All those cases are vital to someone, too, Liam. And they've been waiting longer than you."

Both Jon and Liam began their arguments again, but Molly tuned them out. She hated being in this position; hated having to tell them to wait. She knew the men weren't making demands arbitrarily—what they needed was important. Brows furrowed, she looked down at the items on the table again, began trying to sort through them a little bit. Maybe if she stayed here all night she could get at least a couple of the pieces processed after she finished the cases sitting on her desk.

But which evidence pieces should she process first if she could only get to one or two tonight? In the midst of categorizing the evidence bags in her mind, and placing them in different groups on the table, Molly didn't realize Liam and Jon had stopped pleading their case.

Or that Derek had come to stand right behind her as she sorted through the evidence bags. He reached over and took the bag out of her hand and laid it on the table, and picked up two others near it.

Startled, Molly spun around, then immediately regretted it as she found herself trapped between the evidence table and Derek's hard body. Oh, dear lord. Was she supposed to be able to come up with actual words right now? Something coherent?

Derek took a small step backward, just enough so he could hold one of the evidence bags up between them.

"This one is most important," he said softly, holding up a small bag with what looked like part of a phone or communication device. "Although I know it's partially melted and will be difficult. The other is just the prints from the dead guy to run for ID. Should be simple. Both as soon as you can manage, Molly. But I know your other work here is also important."

Molly just nodded.

Derek hooked a finger into the hip pocket of her lab coat. He took the two small evidence bags and dropped them in. But instead of letting her go as she expected, he placed both hands on her waist.

Molly pretty much forgot how to breathe.

"Thank you," Derek said, his gravelly voice playing havoc with her insides. "I know this means more work for you, and I'm sorry."

"It—it's okay."

"Did you eat dinner?"

"Um, today?"

Derek shook his head and sighed. "I want you to eat something, all right?" His hands tightened the slightest bit on her waist. "You're too tiny as it is."

"Wh-what?" Since when was Derek aware of her eating habits?

"And not the vending machine. A real, proper meal. Promise me you'll go down to the cafeteria tonight and eat something if you're working here a long time."

Molly nodded.

"And not tomorrow morning. Tonight, okay? In the next couple of hours," Derek asked again. "Promise?"

"I promise." Molly forced the words to come out with no stammer.

Derek smiled, and for a second looked as if he was going to say something else, but then Liam and Jon began talking to each other as they repacked the other evidence to be placed on the in-processing shelf. Whatever Derek had been about to say in that moment was gone.

He dropped his hands from Molly's waist and took a step back. "Thanks for processing that communication device tonight. I'm hoping it may be a key piece in the Chicago case."

Without another word, Derek turned and walked out the lab doors. Jon and Liam said their goodbyes as they left, too. Molly finally began breathing normally again.

But as the doors closed, she heard it, although they obviously didn't mean for her to: quiet laughter and the words *Mousy Molly*.

Molly stayed where she was against the evidence table as if glued there. It wasn't Derek who called her mousy, it was never Derek. But it was everyone else. Molly didn't think Jon and Liam meant any harm by the expression, but it was true. Molly *was* mousy in all its elements: nervous, shy, lacking in presence or charisma. Heck even her coloring was mousy: brown eyes, brown hair.

Okay, yeah, it hurt a little bit. Molly didn't want to be mousy. And really most of the time she wasn't that bad. It was just when she was around Derek that she became unbearable to herself.

Molly brought her hands down to her waist where Derek's had been. Derek had actually touched her. That didn't happen very often. Although they saw each other a few times a week, Derek was very careful not to touch her in even the most casual way.

He really hadn't touched her at all since the time he showed up at her condo three years ago—*drunk*—and they'd had sex.

Molly still grimaced when she thought about it. He'd been inebriated, he'd needed a friend. She should've just made a pallet for him on her couch and let him sleep it off.

Instead of taking him to her bed and having the most wonderful night of her life.

Except Derek had been gone when she woke up the next morning. And he had never brought it up again, so she assumed he didn't remember much about that night at all. But Molly did. She also remembered their embrace in the lab about a year ago… The only other time he'd touched her.

Molly sighed and pushed herself off the table. There was no way she was going to start thinking about this again. She had entirely too much work to do. She would put in a call to David, the newest young tech, and see if he was willing to make some extra money by coming back in and helping her with this processing.

There was a lot of important work to do and she planned to get it done. She might be Mousy Molly like the guys said, but there was one thing she knew how to do well: her job.

Chapter Three

Derek cringed when he heard Jon and Liam's Mousy Molly comments as they followed him out the lab doors. How he hated that nickname. He knew the guys didn't really mean any harm by it, neither Jon nor Liam would ever purposely be unkind to someone like Molly, but Derek still hated it.

"I think you probably could've pushed to get more of our evidence processed tonight," Jon said with a little snicker as they walked down the hallway. "I don't know why Liam and I even tried talking to her. We should've used you from the beginning."

"It's not like that, Jon." Derek kept walking, hoping they'd just drop it. They had a meeting with Omega's Critical Response Division Director Steve Drackett in five minutes, teleconference with state officials not long afterward.

Both men laughed. "Uh, it's *exactly* like that. Of course, it's always like that with Molly when it comes to you," Liam told him.

Jon continued, "Yeah, if you had asked her to process *all* our evidence tonight I bet she would've done it. If she could've managed to get a sentence out."

Liam stopped walking and, with a dramatic sigh, grabbed Jon by the waist and pushed him up against the hallway wall. Liam pulled out a pen and held it in front of Jon's face.

Derek stopped to watch the show that was obviously for him.

"Just this one piece of evidence, Molly." Liam deepened his voice to mimic Derek, wiggling the pen and keeping his other hand on Jon's waist.

Jon's falsetto was even more annoying, especially given he was three inches taller than Liam's six-one. "B-but D-Derek, we're s-so busy."

If anything, Liam's voice got even deeper. "Please, Molly. For me? Because I'm Derek Waterman and I'm the best agent in the world."

"For you D-Derek, anything." Derek watched as his two coworkers embraced, then pulled apart, bowing.

Derek raised an eyebrow and just stared at them. "You morons done?"

He started walking down the hallway again.

"Oh, come on, Derek." Jon caught up to him first. "We like Molly as much as anybody. Hell, everybody likes her, she's so sweet and kind. But she gets so awkward around you, it's pretty entertaining."

"Obviously, she's not your type," Liam continued. "That's cool."

"What do you mean she's not my type?" Derek knew he shouldn't let himself get drawn into this conversation, but couldn't help it.

Of course Liam was right, Molly wasn't his type. Molly was sweet, kind, tender, gentle.

Everything Derek knew he should stay away from. Everything he knew he would destroy if he allowed himself near.

"I just mean you're not interested or attracted or whatever. It's obvious by the way I've never even seen you touch her before today." Liam shrugged. "You don't take advantage of her feelings, which is admirable."

Yeah, Derek tried not to touch Molly, because every time he did it went further than he wanted. Like a few minutes ago. He'd touched her waist, and all he could think about was sitting her up on that table and kissing her until neither of them even remembered what the word *evidence* meant.

"Yeah, I wish someone would get that tongue-tied around me," Jon said. "At least you got her to process the important evidence."

"Molly works hard, you guys. She's probably going to be here all night, doing what we asked *plus* all her other stuff. None of us will be working all night. So stow the comments."

That shut them up. Good. Derek needed to drag his focus away from Molly Humphries and back onto this case since they were walking into the director's office.

"Quite a mess today, gentlemen," Steve Drackett, division director, said as he opened his office door and met them in the hallway. "Walk with me on the way to the teleconference room."

"Yeah, it was a mess," Derek told him.

"What happened?" Steve's tone wasn't angry or condescending.

Derek explained what happened this afternoon, about the suspect killing himself and the house being burned to the ground. Since no harm had come to any bystanders, it was a little easier to report.

"So today was both good and bad," Steve said.

"Mostly bad," Jon muttered.

They made it to the conference room door. Derek opened it and they all moved inside. Steve had been giving daily briefings to a group of DC state officials—a committee of congressmen, senators, members of the Department of Defense and Department of Justice—each day since the Chicago bombing. Since Omega Sector's Critical Response Division was a multiagency task force made up of the best people each agency had to offer, faster, better and more detailed results were generally expected. And they were expected from people very high up in the governmental food chain.

So not having those expected results, hell, not having any results at all when they reported every day was getting a little old for everyone.

"We've got just over seven minutes until the call," the technician working the room told them. In seven minutes they would be staring down five different government officials on different screens.

"The only good thing to report about today is that it was at least an actual *live* lead," Derek told Steve. "We've personally followed up dozens since the Chicago attack which have led to nothing. This at least led to something."

Steve nodded. "Yeah, an important something. Critical enough that your suspect would *kill himself* rather than be taken into custody. That's pretty extreme. Do we know who the guy was?"

"Lab is running prints. We'll know in the morning. Local PD should be bringing the body, too."

"Yes, I got a report that the body was on its way, should be here within the hour," Steve told them.

"Hopefully this guy's ID should provide some sort of clue," Liam said, settling himself in a corner that would be out of the way of the cameras. Smart man. "But not as much as having him alive for questioning. Sorry, boss, if I'd had any inclination that he would off himself, I would've tackled him. I thought he might shoot at us, but not himself."

Steve shrugged. "You did the best you could with the info you had. Don't beat yourself up."

One thing Derek liked about having Drackett as his boss was that Steve hadn't been out of the field so long that he'd forgotten that sometimes things just went to hell for no particular reason. Steve was probably only ten years older than Derek's thirty-three years.

"Was anything recovered from the house before the fire completely burned it down?" Steve asked.

"We got out a few potential pieces of evidence. One looked particularly promising. Some sort of communication device. Looks like it could hold pictures or other data, if it can be retrieved," Derek told him, as Steve took notes. "Molly is rush-processing that for us herself tonight."

Jon and Liam made eye contact with each other at that, but Derek ignored them.

"Molly's got to get more people hired in the lab so she's not at Omega twenty hours a day." Steve scribbled something else on his notepad. Derek hoped it was a reminder to talk to Molly so she could get some of the lab workload off her shoulders. She looked tired.

Pretty, as always, but tired.

"What I find most interesting," Derek said, reining in his thoughts, "is that whatever was there, they burnt the building *to the ground* to get rid of it, definitely using an accelerant. The fire was almost as drastic as the guy killing himself."

"Which means you were really close to something," Steve finished for him. "All right, let's present this to the committee."

"One minute until the call, sir," the technician told him.

Steve nodded and looked at Derek. "You ready?"

"Oh, yeah," he answered, rolling his eyes. "Getting chewed out by government officials who really have no idea how to do police work is the favorite part of my day."

"First caller is connecting now," the technician announced. Derek and Steve sat down behind the computer that would show all the people on the call, and also make Derek and Steve visible to them.

And great, it was Congressman Donald Hougland. Always the first person on the video call and the last person off. And always the most vocal about Omega Sector's lack of results with the bombing.

"Gentlemen," Congressman Hougland said. "Hope we have good news today. Or at least not no news at all, as usual."

Derek reminded himself not to roll his eyes because that could be seen by the other man.

"Congressman Hougland." Steve was a much better diplomat so Derek let him talk. "We're just waiting for the others, and we'll provide an update. We've had a breakthrough. I believe you'll be pleased."

"I doubt it," the older man said. "For an organization that's supposed to be stellar, I've yet to see evidence of that. Of course, I've yet to see evidence of anything." He laughed at his own joke.

Thankfully, the other committee members chose that moment to connect to the conference call so Derek could force himself to swallow his tart retort for Congressman Hougland.

Derek had been raised on a ranch in Wyoming by his reluctant, confirmed-bachelor uncle when Derek's parents had died when he was twelve. So cursing had been a prevalent part of his upbringing.

But telling a US congressman to kiss his ass was probably not going to help any part of this conference call or overall situation. He could see Steve looking over at him cautiously as if preparing to kick him under the table if he opened his mouth. Derek glanced at him and nodded to let him know he wasn't going to do anything stupid.

The head of the committee, and much more amiable, Senator Edmundson, opened the conference. "Director Drackett, Agent Waterman, thank you for speaking with us today. We know your time is valuable."

"Senator," Steve responded respectfully. "Ladies and gentlemen."

"Let's cut to the chase, Robert," Congressman Hougland said, practically cutting off Steve's greeting to the committee. "Drackett mentioned they have some news. I'd be thrilled to hear that." Sarcasm dripped from his words.

Annoyance floated over Senator Edmundson's face before he reschooled it into its polite mask.

"All right, then. Director Drackett, please."

"Agent Waterman and his colleagues received a tip earlier today while returning from Chicago. They changed route midflight and headed to Philadelphia. Upon their arrival at the location, they were met with gunfire."

The men and women were listening attentively from their screens. It made for a nice change from the past two weeks when they'd had nothing of any interest to report.

"One man gave chase, and unfortunately killed himself rather than be taken into custody," Steve continued. "The suspects also burned the location to the ground while the team was chasing the running suspect."

"So basically, Agent Waterman, you had a more exciting day, but still have nothing to show for it," Congressman Hougland jumped in. "Is that correct?"

Derek counted to three before answering. He'd once been thrown from a spooked horse and had to walk the four miles home on a broken ankle. He'd survived that.

He could survive this.

"Actually, Congressman, we were able to retrieve a few pieces of evidence from the house before it was totally destroyed. One piece in particular, a communication device of some kind, looks particularly interesting. Although it was damaged by the fire, we're hopeful the data on it can be retrieved."

Most of the committee were nodding, at least accepting that this was progress. Not Hougland.

"Hopeful," he scoffed. "Not exactly confidence-inspiring."

"All right, Don, let's stay positive," Senator Edmundson said.

"The only thing I'm becoming positive about is that Omega Sector might not be living up to its reputation any longer," Hougland spat back.

Derek's lips thinned. As much as he disliked the congressman, the man wasn't totally incorrect. He and the team had been pretty inept on this Chicago case. They hadn't caught a single break until today.

"We should also have identification of the dead man soon," Drackett told the committee. "That will also point us in a direction."

"The body is there now, at your facility in Colorado?" Senator Edmundson asked.

Steve nodded. "Yes, our lab is or very soon will be, running the prints. We'll also have any other helpful evidence from the body."

"And the communication device? When will you know if that will provide anything useful?" Hougland asked.

"By tomorrow morning," Derek replied. He hoped that would be true. "The lab is working on it tonight."

That seemed to placate everyone. Since there weren't any other questions from the committee and Hougland had evidently gotten tired of poking holes at their case, Steve said good-night to everyone, promising to keep them posted. After the last of the committee had disconnected from the screens, Derek ran a weary hand over his face.

Jon and Liam stood up from their chairs in the corner.

"I am so glad I'm not you guys," Jon said. "That was brutal."

Derek couldn't agree more. He just wanted to get home, change out of his smoky clothes and shower. The burns on his back and shoulders were still bothering him a little. Everyone said their good-nights, agreeing to meet back first thing in the morning.

Derek partly wanted to go check on Molly, but decided it was better to just let her work on her own since his presence tended to discombobulate her so much. But he hated that she had more work on her plate—probably a whole night's worth—because of him. Derek promised himself that when this case was over, he would make sure that Steve forced Molly to hire some more people for the lab.

He needed a good night's sleep. Once they had this evidence in hand, it would hopefully lead them somewhere, and they'd all need to be able to hit the ground running. Derek was still thinking about the evidence through his meal, shower and even as he was falling asleep. Why would someone kill himself rather than be arrested? What was on that device that was worth burning a building to the ground? Molly's results would point them in the direction they needed to go. He drifted off to sleep with it on his mind.

The phone ringing at 2:42 a.m. jerked him out of his sleep. This was not the first call he'd gotten from Omega in the middle of the night. Derek looked at the caller ID: Steve Drackett.

"Steve, what's up?" Derek tried to wipe the sleep from his voice the best he could.

"Derek, I need you to get back to HQ right away. There's been an explosion at the building. I'm on my way in now, but you're closer."

Derek was instantly awake. "Like what, a fire?"

"No. I don't have many details yet, but I know it was an explosion. In the forensic lab."

Derek could actually feel his heart stop beating. "Forensic lab?" he parroted.

"Yes. And I know there's at least one confirmed death."

Chapter Four

Derek's general idea of "help from above" was a sniper on the roof, but he prayed like he had never prayed before as he broke multiple traffic laws driving back to Omega Headquarters in downtown Colorado Springs.

It was nearly three in the morning. The forensic lab had just exploded. One person was dead.

No matter how much he tried to twist it, there was no way to think that it wasn't Molly. Who else would even be there at almost three o'clock in the morning?

Acid ate at his gut when Derek thought of the fact that she wouldn't have been there at all if he hadn't asked her to stay. To do something specifically for him.

But he categorically refused to assume the worst until there was no other choice. Until he was presented with proof positive that it was Molly who was dead.

He hit the gas harder and rounded a corner, nearly blinded by all the emergency vehicle lights parked at Omega. A uniformed officer stopped him from pulling into the parking lot, but let Derek through when he flashed his badge and ID.

Which saved Derek from having to pull his gun on the man. Because there was no way in hell he wasn't getting into that parking lot.

Chaos reigned as Derek parked his car far enough away

not to hinder any emergency vehicles and jogged over to a small group of personnel who seemed to be directing the efforts.

Behind them he could see the building burning, the concentration of flames largest in the southwest corner. Smoke billowed from right where the forensic lab was located—what was left of it.

"I'm Omega agent Derek Waterman, standing in for Director Drackett until he gets here in a few minutes." Derek pulled out his ID, but the men barely glanced at it.

"Captain Jim Brandal, with Station 433," the man closest to Derek, holding a hand radio, said, nodding at him. "You've had some sort of explosion in the southwest corner of the building."

"That's the forensic lab." Derek kept the panic out of his voice.

Captain Brandal looked over at the man standing next to him and both of their faces turned more grim. "That's what we figured. Any hazardous materials there?"

Derek shrugged. He was sure there were, but he didn't know what. "Almost definitely. You have one confirmed dead?" His throat tightened as he said the words.

"Yes," Captain Brandal agreed, and then started to say more before stopping to respond to a report from the radio in his hand.

Derek shifted in frustration. Who was dead? Where? Had the ID of the victim been established?

But looking at the smoke from the forensic lab, so much more than from the house fire today that had been minutes from taking his own life, Derek realized no one could've survived in there.

Derek steeled himself, forced himself to cut off emotions altogether. It was one of the things he'd become an expert at over the years.

The fire department captain turned back to Derek after his radio conversation. "Sorry. Yes, one confirmed dead. But the good news is that the fire doors in the building instantly shut after the explosion. So there should be very limited causalities outside of the immediate blast site."

Some part of Derek knew that was good, but the biggest part of him didn't care if everyone else in the building survived if Molly had died. He managed to nod at Captain Brandal.

Brandal continued, "Based on what the firefighters closest to the blaze reported, it looks like there was an explosion in the lab, which is why we asked about hazardous materials."

"I'm sure there were flammable items in the lab, but the safety record there is exemplary. Never been any problems reported whatsoever," Derek told the man.

He had a hard time imagining meticulous Molly being anything but completely safe in her lab. But she was overworked and overtired. Anyone could make a mistake under those conditions.

The Captain shrugged. "It only takes one time."

Derek felt guilt threaten to overtake him as the man's words echoed his thoughts. But he ruthlessly tamped it down. There'd be time for guilt later. Right now he had to know the answer to the question burning a hole in his gut.

"Has the body been identified yet?" he asked through gritted teeth. Then an ugly thought hit him. "Can it even be identified here on scene?"

Maybe there wasn't enough left of the body to be identified visually. The thought made him sick to his stomach.

"Hang on." Captain Brandal spoke into the radio again and waited for a response. "The body is over by the paramedics. I'm sorry for your loss, but truly, with an explosion of this size, it's nothing short of a miracle that only one life was lost."

Nothing felt further from the truth to Derek. He wiped a hand over his face. "Thanks," he murmured.

"Paramedics said you should probably be able to ID the guy visually. If not, we can use other means."

Derek's head jerked up. "*Guy*? Paramedics are sure the victim is a man?"

Brandal spoke into his radio once again, then turned back to Derek. "Yep. Young black male. Midtwenties."

Definitely not Molly. Derek felt relief flood through him.

But where was she?

THE EXPLOSION ROCKED the whole building. Molly had been staring at the vending machine in the break room outside the lab, feeling guilty because she had promised Derek she would eat hours ago in the cafeteria, when she found herself thrown back against the wall and crumpling to the ground.

For long, panicked moments she couldn't hear, couldn't see. She struggled to get her bearings, feeling around along the floor. The emergency generator lights kicked on, casting a ghoulish gray light around the break room. But at least she could see.

The vending machine lay broken on the floor, the chairs and table knocked over and scattered across the room. The coffeemaker was hanging precariously off the side of a shelf, held by just its cord plugged into the wall. Dust floated around everywhere, like snowflakes in slow motion, moving in all directions.

Molly began moving toward the hallway, trying to shake off the ringing in her ears. What had happened?

Not an earthquake. It was too loud. Definitely some sort of explosion.

She needed to get back to the lab, but once she rounded the corner from the break room she realized the lab was on fire. In all the chaos it took her longer than it normally would've to realize that the explosion had come *from* the lab.

Oh, no. David had been working in there.

Molly rushed forward, but after only a few feet ran into the clear fire wall. It had automatically lowered, as it was meant to do, to keep damage from spreading. Looking into the area where the lab had once stood, she knew there was no way the young tech had made it out of there alive.

And if the explosion had happened five minutes earlier, Molly would've been in there with David.

She knew if this door was closed, others around the building would be, too. All she could do was wait for the firefighters to do their job. She sat back on the floor and tried to figure out what had happened. Her ears were still ringing and the room still seemed to spin slightly.

Had something in the lab caused the fire? There were always hazardous materials around, but everyone who worked there—including David—was trained in lab safety. She couldn't think of anything they'd been working on that could've caused something this damaging, but right now it was too hard to even get her thoughts straight.

And, oh gosh, David was probably dead.

Molly just closed her eyes and leaned her head back against the wall. Eventually rescue workers came through and led her out. They wrapped her in a blanket and she was now sitting in the back of an ambulance. Still dazed.

She had been questioned multiple times. What did she think had caused the explosion? What hazardous elements had been in active use in the lab? Had there been anyone else working besides herself and David?

She answered each time as best she could about the causes, but just like when she had been sitting inside, she couldn't figure out what would have triggered an explosion of that magnitude.

And no, no one else had been there besides her and David. The young man's death had already been confirmed.

She didn't know what to do, who to call. It was even more chaotic and loud out here than it had been inside near the explosion. The rescue workers were all moving at a brisk pace, yelling to one another, coordinating the best they could to do their job.

Molly liked order and quiet, not the cacophony of havoc currently swirling around her. She resisted the urge to put her hands over her ears and close her eyes.

And then she saw him.

Derek was walking directly toward her, determination in his eyes. He radiated a definite purpose in his walk, because no one got in his way; instead, they stepped around him. He didn't stop until he was right in front of her.

She wanted to jump into his arms, to beg him to take her from here. But this was Derek Waterman. Jumping into his arms wasn't an option.

She was shocked when he put his large hands on either side of her head and tilted her head back so she was looking into his blue eyes, and found them searching her face intently.

"Are you okay?" His voice was deep, gravelly. "Injured?"

"No, I'm fine. But David Thompson, the new lab assistant, is dead, Derek." Molly could feel herself begin to cry.

To her shock, Derek pulled her to his chest and wrapped his arms around her.

"I know. I identified the body a few minutes ago."

She leaned into Derek's strength. He'd never put his arms around her in public before, but Molly didn't question it. She needed his strength right now.

"I heard they'd found a body in the lab and I thought it was you, Molls. How did you get out?"

"I wasn't in there when the explosion happened. I'd gone out to get something to eat." She leaned back from his chest so she could look at him. "Like you told me to do."

"I told you to do it hours ago." He pulled her back against his chest. "Thank God you suck at following directions."

Everything going on around her, all the noise and chaos, all the danger, didn't seem quite so overwhelming against Derek's chest. "Actually, I'm quite good at following directions," she murmured. "I just lost track of time."

She heard him chuckle before confirming with the paramedic that she hadn't sustained any injuries needing further medical treatment.

"Oh, thank God!" Molly found herself ripped out of Derek's arms and hugged against the even larger chest of Jon Hatton. "You cannot believe how glad I am to see you, Molly."

Molly liked Jon just fine. And heaven knew he was attractive enough—six-four of solid gorgeousness—but right now she just wanted to jump out of the man's embrace and back into Derek's. But the moment had passed. Derek had turned to talk to Director Drackett and wasn't even looking her way anymore.

As if it had never happened.

As usual.

"Are you okay, honey?" Jon released her from his hug,

but kept one arm around her. "When we heard someone from the lab was dead…"

"David Thompson. The new tech." Sadness filled her again. Nobody that young should die.

"I'm sorry, kiddo." Jon squeezed her before letting her go. "But I'm glad it wasn't you."

As she stood watching the firefighters put the last of the flames out, Molly knew how lucky she'd been. And although she was heartbroken over David, she was glad it hadn't been her, too.

Chapter Five

Derek was listening to what Steve Drackett was saying while trying to force himself not to punch Jon in the face. Seriously, the man had been his colleague and one of his closest friends for over five years, but when he had snatched Molly out of his arms and into his own...

Derek reminded himself that Jon had no romantic intentions toward Molly. And even if he did, Molly was free to date whomever she wanted. Derek had no claim on her.

But damned if he wasn't totally relieved when Molly stepped away from Jon. Derek pretended not to pay any attention to them whatsoever as he spoke with his boss. But he knew exactly where Molly was.

Of course, he always knew where Molly was if she was anywhere in his vicinity. It was as if he had an internal radar set solely for her. Not that he could do anything but keep a watchful eye on her. Anything else wasn't acceptable.

"Based on the preliminary report, the fire department feels like it was definitely something from the lab that detonated. Not caught on fire. Actually blew up," Derek told Steve. "One confirmed death. Protection walls came down, so it looks like other damage and causalities are pretty minimal."

The director nodded, then turned to Molly. "You okay?"

"Not physically hurt. But sick about David's death." Molly's voice was strained. Derek had to resist the urge to wrap an arm around her again.

The one good thing about the trauma of the explosion was that it seemed to have made Molly forget to be nervous around him. At least she wasn't stammering.

"Can you give us a report? Do you know what happened?" Steve asked her.

"We were working." Molly shrugged one delicate shoulder. "Nothing out of the ordinary. Our caseload had heightened, so I called David and asked him to come back in. But we weren't working with anything hazardous or explosive."

Molly ran a hand over her face, exhausted. "I'm sorry." Her voice was shaky. "I'm trying to figure out what it could've been. But I don't think it was anything we were working on. I—" She rubbed a hand over her face again.

"Molly, it's okay," Jon said to her, coming to stand close to her again. "We'll get it all worked out. I'm sure it wasn't your fault."

Molly just shook her head, her hand still covering her face.

Jon looked at Derek and Steve, then tilted his head in Molly's direction. He wanted to take her home. She obviously needed to go and really couldn't help anything here.

But over Derek's dead body was Jon taking Molly anywhere. Derek would take her home.

Derek walked over to Molly and touched her gently on the arm. The arm that had been covering her face dropped to her side. Her eyes seemed glassy, dazed.

"Hey." He bent at the knees so they could be eye to eye. He tucked an errant strand of her long brown hair back behind her ear. "I'm going to take you home, okay? We'll figure out what happened tomorrow."

She nodded, swaying slightly toward him. Derek wrapped

an arm around her shoulders. He looked back at the guys, ignoring both of their slightly shocked expressions at how he was treating Molly.

Maybe he'd made too much of a show out of never touching her over the past couple years.

"I'm going to put her in the car and will be right back. She needs to sit down before she falls down." Both men nodded, their gazes flickering to Molly, where she was tucked under his arm. "I'll take her home in a minute."

Steve stepped up to Molly. "Get some rest, okay? We'll work out what happened later. But I have no question that you will be totally exonerated of all blame."

Molly nodded, but didn't say a word. Derek walked her over to his car and opened the passenger door, thankful for the balmy May night that wasn't too hot or cold. But Molly was shivering slightly, so he grabbed a blazer he had thrown in the backseat and put it around her. He knew her reaction was from shock more than cold, but she wouldn't know the difference.

Once he had her settled in the car, he squatted down so he could look in her eyes again. Hers were still pretty unfocused.

"Hey." He wrapped the jacket more securely around her, then grabbed it by the lapels to bring her in a little closer. "I'm just going to finish my conversation with Steve and Jon and then I'll take you home, okay? Five minutes."

She nodded.

Derek kissed her forehead, then closed the door, jogging back toward Jon and Steve who were walking toward his car. Both of them were still looking at him with odd expressions.

"What?" he barked when they didn't say anything.

"Nothing." Jon shook his head. "Just wondering how I

can call myself a behavioral analyst and miss certain facts that are right before my eyes."

"What are you talking about?"

Jon shook his head again. "Absolutely nothing. Is Molly okay?"

Derek glanced back at his car. "Exhausted. A little shaky. Not unexpected, given the circumstances."

"I believe her when she says that they didn't have any flammable materials out in the lab at the explosion site. Molly's record is impeccable when it comes to safety. Hell, when it comes to anything," Steve stated.

"But she's been working long hours. Was tired. Could've made a mistake she wouldn't normally have." Derek's grim expression matched the other men's.

The director nodded. "And if that's the case, we'll deal with it. I share in that responsibility."

Jon turned and looked back at the building. "But if human error or some other accident wasn't the cause of the explosion, then we have to think about what is."

"What are you thinking? That it was some sort of attack against Omega?" Derek asked.

"Maybe not so much attack as sabotage," Jon responded.

Each man processed that for a minute.

"It seems a little extreme, I know," Jon continued.

"Until you take into consideration someone killing himself rather than being questioned, and perps burning that house to the ground today to keep evidence out of our hands," Derek finished for him.

"Exactly."

Derek grimaced. "Whatever we took into evidence must have been pretty important to blow up the whole damn lab for it."

Steve had been quiet up until now. "And if this is all

connected, then we also have to think about who knew we had that specific evidence here." He shook his head.

"Nobody really knew, but us," Derek said. "Unless you think we have some sort of mole?"

There had been moles in other divisions of Omega Sector in the past. But the Critical Response Division was not a clandestine section of Omega. They worked out in the open, not generally undercover or in the shadows. And although they didn't talk publicly about investigations, Derek had no idea why a terrorist would keep a mole inside the Critical Response Division. Information was pretty open there.

"Not necessarily, at least not within our division," Steve responded. "But perhaps amongst the people we've been reporting to every day."

"The government committee?" Derek asked.

"Actually, I was thinking about that very fact last night, after Congressman Hougland was giving you a hard time," Jon said. Derek wasn't surprised to hear his friend doing what he did best as a behavioral analyst: piecing everything together.

"What did you come up with?" Steve asked.

"Like we've already talked about—obviously there was critical information at the location yesterday, based on the lengths the suspects were willing to go to try and keep us from getting it."

Both Derek and Steve nodded.

"This lead was also unique because we weren't here at Omega when you got the info, Derek. We were in the air following up on something else and switched our focus to the new lead."

They'd been on one of the small Omega jets traveling back to Colorado from a lead in Chicago.

"Yeah, that's true. We moved quicker on this lead than we have some of the others," Derek agreed.

"We also didn't follow exact protocol since we were already out. We hadn't called in our exact location, just decided to go to Philly, and then the building, immediately, since the option was available."

Derek was beginning to see the pattern Jon was suggesting. "Unlike every other lead we've investigated for the last two weeks. Where we've followed protocol pretty much to the letter. And all have led to nothing."

Steve grimaced. "You're thinking sabotage." It wasn't a question.

Jon shrugged. "It's hard to believe that every single lead we've followed has been completely dead. Although I guess that's possible."

"No, I agree with Jon," Derek told Steve. "Sometimes it felt like the people we were after were one step ahead of us. Almost ready for us."

They'd had the normal factions attempt to take credit for the bombing, both international and domestic groups. All had been investigated and all had come to naught. Then all other aspects of the investigation—the bomb site, witnesses, the type of explosions—had also led nowhere.

Maybe everything had led nowhere because someone was deliberately running interference on the perpetrators' behalf.

There were very few people who could have done that effectively. A dirty agent inside the Critical Response Division could, but having one there was unlikely.

And since Derek and this investigation had been under such close scrutiny by high-ranking government officials, any one of them could be responsible, too. Which was uglier, but made more sense in a lot of ways.

"Gentlemen," Steve said. "It looks like there's every

possibility that we've got some high-ranking US official who is tied in with the Chicago terrorist attack."

Jon pointed at the now-destroyed lab. "And we're looking at the third extreme example of what that person, or people, might be willing to do to keep us from making any progress on the case."

"Whoever it is has also put us back at square one in terms of evidence." Derek could feel his teeth grinding, knowing they'd been so close to a real breakthrough only to lose it. "Nothing in the lab survived that explosion. It was definitely important, but now it's gone."

All three men looked at the smoke still rising from the building. The fire was out, but the smoke would linger for a while.

"Well, they may have successfully destroyed whatever evidence we'd gotten yesterday, but they also tipped their hand a little too far," Jon said. "They've given us an edge they don't know we have by revealing they have inside knowledge. We should use that to our advantage."

The director nodded at both men. "I agree. I'm going to start keeping much more careful track of what information is going to which offices. The committee we report to every day hasn't been the only ones requesting information. I'll see what I can narrow down. And I damn sure won't be sharing actual pertinent info about the case any longer."

Steve turned away from the lab. "Go home, get some rest," he continued. "Tomorrow you guys head back out to the house in West Philly, see if anything there can be salvaged. Track down where the lead came from and see if you can get any further info."

Derek nodded. He needed to get Molly home, let her rest. But then he'd be coming right back, or at least working out of his house. Sleep could wait for him. He glanced over at Jon and knew the other man felt the same way.

"I'll let you know when the building is open," Steve said. "This fire is meant not only to destroy evidence, but to misdirect us. Give us a lot of other stuff to be worrying about. We're not going to let that happen."

"Damn right we're not," Jon said.

Some of the firefighters were beginning to pack up their equipment.

"I've got to go sign off on all this," Drackett said, shaking his head. "I'll see you later."

He began walking toward the fire trucks, but then turned back. "And boys, watch your backs. If this goes as high up as I'm afraid it might, we all have targets on us."

Derek nodded. He could feel it, too.

He got back into the car and looked over at Molly. She was sitting in the exact position as when he had left, staring straight out the windshield.

"You doing okay?"

"Yeah." She finally nodded. "I'm just trying to go over in my mind if anything we had out in the lab could've caused this."

He wasn't sure if he should tell her that it might have been a deliberate attack. "Molly, we're looking into a lot of possibilities for what happened. But believe me, no one is assuming you're at fault. You run a pretty tight ship in that lab."

She seemed to relax just a little bit. "Everyone's safety is always my first priority."

"I know that. Everyone knows that."

She seemed tiny inside his blazer, huddled in the seat as he drove out of the Omega parking lot and toward her house.

"You know where I live, right?" she said in a small voice.

Did he know where she lived? Was she kidding? He was guilty of driving by her condo sometimes even when it was almost the opposite direction of the way he needed to go.

And every single time he wanted to stop and knock on her door like that one night three years ago.

Knowing she wouldn't slam the door in his face, wouldn't tell him to go to hell, was the only thing that kept him from doing so. She was too gentle, too kind, too soft to send him away.

And he wasn't so much of a bastard that he was willing to drag her down into the dark world he lived in. He didn't want her touched by the ugliness of the sordid things he'd seen and done.

But damned if that wasn't the hardest thing he'd ever done.

"Yeah, I know where you live."

He could almost see the flush move up her cheeks.

"I just mean… The one time you were there you were… not your normal self. A-and I just wondered."

"Hey." He reached over and grabbed her hand. "You've gone the entire evening without being nervous around me."

"That's because I was upset."

"Then stay upset, at me if you need to. No need to go back to nervous."

She shrugged. He knew he made her nervous, made her uncomfortable.

Just like he knew the way she looked at him when she thought he couldn't see. And he cherished it even as he tried to keep himself distant from it.

Her condo wasn't far from Omega Headquarters and soon he pulled up and into her parking space. She was already opening her door when he came around to help her.

"I'm okay," she said, and although her voice was soft,

it wasn't shaky. "Thanks for the ride. My purse was in the lab with my keys in it. Let me get the spare."

He watched as she hunted around her bushes, and saw her pull it out from where she had used electrical tape to attach it to the main branch. Much better than just slipping it under a front doormat.

"Found it!" The small victory had evidently thrilled her.

"May I?" He took the key when she offered it and opened the door for her. "Do you have another set inside?"

"Yes. This is just for true emergencies."

"Okay, I'll put it back out for you." He slipped it into his pocket.

She stood there in the doorway swamped in his jacket, plaster in her hair, smelling like smoke, smiling her slightly awkward smile that always seemed to be uniquely for him.

She was the most beautiful thing he'd ever seen.

All the lecturing he'd given himself on the drive here about not dragging her down into his darkness completely vanished.

Molly was alive and he had to taste her.

He slipped one arm around her small waist under his jacket and threaded his other hand through the hair at her scalp underneath her long brown braid. He backed her up against the door frame and brought his lips down to hers.

He heard her soft gasp of surprise and took advantage of it to slip his tongue into her mouth. A knot of need twisted inside him as he drew her closer. He felt her arms wrap around his neck as her tongue dueled with his.

His jacket falling from her shoulders and pooling at their feet brought some sense of reality back to Derek.

This could not happen. As much as he wanted it to.

He dropped both hands to her waist and took a step back. "Molly..."

She blinked up at him, arms still around his neck.

"Molly, this isn't a good idea."

"Why?" She leaned forward again.

Hell if he could remember why in this moment. Her lips were almost to his. If he kissed her again he wasn't sure he would have the strength to stop. "You have plaster in your hair."

"What?"

"Plaster. It's all in your hair."

Her face that had just been so flushed and soft from his kisses became shuttered. Her arms dropped to her sides, before one came up to her head to find the plaster he had mentioned. Why the hell had he said that? He didn't care about anything being in her hair. He'd just meant that she had been through a trauma and that they shouldn't do anything she might regret.

Or he might regret. Like break her heart.

"Oh. Yeah. I—I probably need a shower pretty badly."

The thought of Molly in the shower had everything in Derek's body tightening, but the slight stutter wasn't lost on him. He hated that he'd made her uncomfortable around him again. And her eyes were wounded.

Damn it. He had to get out of here just to stop the damage he was inflicting.

"I'll pick you up tomorrow at nine, okay?" He glanced down at his watch. "Actually, that's only about four hours from now, so let's make it ten. You'll need to give an official report."

Molly nodded and stepped inside her door. She picked up his jacket and held it out to him, wary, as if she didn't know what to expect.

Derek didn't blame her. He couldn't run more hot and cold if he tried.

He took the blazer from her. "Just get some rest. It's been a crazy day for all of us."

He waited until she closed the door—without a word—then turned and walked back to his car.

Damn it.

Chapter Six

It's been a crazy day for all of us.

Molly turned on the shower water to let it warm up. She slipped her lab coat off as well as her other clothes, all of which smelled like smoke, and just threw them in the bathtub so they wouldn't contaminate her clothes in the hamper.

She glanced briefly in the mirror before stepping into her walk-in shower. Yeah, she did have some plaster in her hair.

But let's face it, Derek could've had giant pieces of cement or paint or a dozen more building substances covering his entire head and Molly would've kept kissing him.

That was the difference between them.

Derek Waterman was out of her league and she needed to remember that. He was glad she was alive and had kissed her. But tomorrow they'd be back to their same old routine: him acting as if nothing had ever happened between them and her acting like a complete nincompoop around him.

As Molly washed the mess from the explosion off her body and out of her hair, she decided it was time to stop the silly way she'd been acting around him all this time. She was a strong, intelligent woman. She needed to act that way.

She completely ignored that she had made that promise to herself multiple times before. This time she was going to do it.

Plus, she had other things to worry about besides Derek Waterman and his kisses. She got out of the shower and dried off, slipping on a pair of yoga pants and a T-shirt, rebraiding her hair.

The explosion in the lab. She rubbed a hand over her face as she walked downstairs to get something to eat. Even if the explosion wasn't her fault, the workload resulting from it would be enormous. Sorting through which evidence was completely destroyed, or whether any of it could be salvaged, would be a daunting task.

Without a doubt many Omega cases would be ruined because of what had happened tonight. Crimes would go unsolved, some criminals unpunished. It was frustrating to consider.

Molly made herself a sandwich, poured herself a glass of milk and forced herself to finish both even though she didn't want to. She was going to need her strength for tomorrow and a full stomach would help her get rest now.

All of the findings for past cases had been backed up on a server in a different building, just in case of a situation like what had happened tonight. But current cases... They would have to be sorted through individually. And almost all findings would now be ineligible in court because they had been contaminated.

Worst of all, a young man—a promising young life—had perished.

Molly got up and put her dishes in the sink and stood there for just a moment, head hanging low. How she hoped they could prove this wasn't her fault. She didn't know how she was going to live with herself otherwise.

For the first time Molly wished she was a drinker. That

she had some sort of hard liquor in the house that she could use to help alleviate all these thoughts in her head just for tonight. Be drunk and just not care.

And maybe, just maybe, she would go show up at Derek's house drunk. And they could have sex again. Turnabout was fair play, after all.

Who was she kidding? Like she'd ever have the guts. She'd be thrilled if she could just talk to him like a normal person tomorrow when he came to pick her up. Which was just a few hours from now. She should get some sleep because she was obviously slap happy, thinking about drinking and having sex with Derek.

She went back into her bathroom to brush her teeth and took another look at herself in the mirror. No plaster in her hair, it was all tidy in its braid. Would Derek mention their kiss when he saw her tomorrow or pretend like it never happened? Again. She was interested to find out.

Crossing into her bedroom, she stopped as she realized the door leading to her small balcony was cracked open. Molly racked her brain. Had she opened it when she first got home? Had it been open when she got into the shower earlier? It was a nice night and now that she wasn't in shock she wasn't feeling so cold. But she still didn't sleep with doors open.

As she crossed to shut it, she saw movement out of the corner of her eye and gasped. *Someone was in the room with her.*

She opened her mouth to scream when the arm of a different, second person came around her head and covered her mouth roughly.

"She saw you. Get the drug. Hurry up," one voice whispered to the other.

Molly began to struggle as hard as she could, throwing her weight back and twisting in the arms that held her. The hand squeezed harder on her face and jerked her head to the side, exposing her neck.

She felt a sharp prick in her neck as the second man injected her with something.

Molly fought to keep her head, to not panic. Whatever they had injected her with would only work faster if she was flailing around. She couldn't fight them both anyway.

She let her body go slack.

"That was fast. Is that how it works?" the second man asked the first.

"How the hell should I know? Let's get her to the car. The plane will be waiting for us." Voice number one.

Plane? Oh God, where were they taking her? Molly struggled to focus over the effect of the drug they'd given her. One man grabbed her feet and the other carried her torso as they took her downstairs, then out the back through her sliding glass door. Molly tried to make her body respond once they got outside. If she was going to try to flee, now would be the best time.

But she couldn't make her body respond as they threw her in the backseat of their car parked right outside her gate. She watched her row of condos get smaller from the window.

She wasn't sure how long the car had been moving, and she definitely had no idea which direction they'd been going when it stopped again. But she could see an airplane hangar and small runway. Not the Denver airport, a much smaller regional one.

Through the fog of her mind Molly figured out that this was her only chance. Once they had her on a plane she'd have no opportunity to escape. The movement would send the drug faster through her bloodstream, but she couldn't wait. And even in the haze she could imagine the terrible things they would do to her.

The men were arguing in the front seat, about something she couldn't begin to understand, obviously not thinking her a threat of any kind. Using all her focus, she opened the door of the car and poured herself through the opening.

She tried to stand upright to run, but the world was spinning too rapidly. In a sort of three-limbed crawl-run she moved as rapidly as she could toward the tree line surrounding the airstrip.

She couldn't hear anything but her own breathing, sobs coming from her chest as she tried to force her body to move faster. Her vision blurred as the drug took greater affect.

For just a moment she was sure she was going to make it. Then a hand grabbed her shoulder, spinning her around and sending her sprawling to the ground. She felt the pin prick again, this time in her arm.

"You're tricky." It was the first man. The one she had seen in her apartment. "But that should do it."

The other man, the angry one, came up next to him. "I'll take care of this the old-fashioned way."

Molly tried to move away from his fist flying at her, but there was nowhere to go and she couldn't get her body to move anyway.

She felt a pain like she'd never known against her jaw, then everything went blessedly black.

DEREK HAD GONE back to Omega Headquarters after dropping Molly off. But Steve had sent both him and Jon home. There was nothing that could be done until all the firefighters were cleared out, and they'd both be more useful after a few hours of sleep.

Molly's house was much closer and Derek was tempted to stop there and catch a few hours of sleep on her couch.

Except he knew there would be no sleeping or couching going on if he did.

So he'd headed back to his own house and spent the couple of remaining hours of the morning trying, not very successfully, to sleep. And trying, again totally unsuccessfully, not to think about that kiss in Molly's doorway.

Or her face when he'd stopped it and told her it was because she had plaster in her hair, for God's sake. This was a shining example of why he shouldn't be with her.

He was too rough and she was too gentle. She would always end up getting hurt around him.

But now he was on his way back to her house to pick Molly up. They both had long, hard days ahead of them.

And so help him, if she still had that sad look of rejection in her eyes when he saw her, Derek didn't know if he'd be able to stop himself from taking her to bed right then and there to prove how much he wanted her. Consequences be damned.

He couldn't stand the thought of her thinking he didn't want her. Because he did. Every moment of every day. But he knew he wasn't good for her. More than not good for her.

Poison for her.

He pulled up at her house and knocked on the door just a couple minutes before ten o'clock. When there was no answer he knocked again.

Nothing.

Had he gotten the time wrong?

Or maybe Molly had finally come to her senses and decided she didn't want to be around him anymore. He couldn't blame her for that. But he still wanted to make sure she was okay. He wished he could call her, but knew her phone had been destroyed in the lab.

He grabbed his phone and called Jon.

"Hey, you on your way in?" Jon answered without pre-amble. "I'm already here. It's still pretty much chaos."

"Have you seen Molly around or heard from her? I thought I was supposed to pick her up this morning but she's not answering her door."

"No, I haven't seen her, but that doesn't mean she's not here. Let me check with Drackett."

Derek stepped back so he could get a better look at her condo. None of the windows had any drapes open. If she had already left, then she hadn't taken the time to open any blinds first.

"Steve hasn't seen her, either. I don't think she's here, man."

"Okay. I'll see if I can find her." No need to panic yet. "I'll be in soon."

Derek still had her extra key from last night, since he'd been so hell-bent on getting out of there as fast as possible. He knocked harder on the door, but when he received no answer again after a few seconds, he let himself inside.

"Molly? Are you here? I'm coming in." He had been in law enforcement long enough to know not to enter a building unannounced if you weren't on some sort of covert op.

He stopped just inside the doorway to listen for any sounds that would give away Molly's presence: a shower, hair dryer, dishwasher. But there was nothing but silence.

"Molls?" Derek was actually worried now, running through possible scenarios in his head. What if she had been more hurt from the fire than any of them had thought?

He checked her bedroom first, then the bathroom and guest room. Back downstairs he found a dish in the sink, with crumbs from what looked to have been a sandwich. An interesting breakfast choice.

She wasn't here and her bed was made. Which meant

she either hadn't slept in it at all or had already gotten up and was on her way.

Maybe she really was mad at him and had made her way to Omega on her own. Or maybe she just hadn't been able to sleep and decided to go in to HQ where she could do some good.

It wasn't like her to be inconsiderate, but she didn't have a phone to contact him.

There were a lot of reasons why she could be out of pocket. All of them perfectly reasonable. But something about this wasn't sitting right in Derek's gut.

And he knew it wouldn't ease until he found her.

Chapter Seven

Derek didn't waste any time getting back to Omega Headquarters. He hoped Molly would be there, even if she was mad and didn't want to talk to him. At least he would know she was safe.

The scene at Omega was less hectic than the night before. All the rescue vehicles and personnel were gone. Like the fire department captain had said, most of the damage had been contained to the forensic lab. The fire doors had saved the rest of the building.

Derek checked with security first. Everyone had to log in to enter the building. There was no record of Molly's entry. Derek made his way to the main group of offices where his desk was located. The offices were far enough from last night's fire to still be operational. Everywhere he looked, Omega agents were doing their normal jobs. Fighting crime and keeping society safe didn't stop just because of a setback. Even one as large as last night's fire.

"Did you find Molly?" Derek wasn't even to his desk before Jon caught up with him.

"No. You haven't seen her anywhere around here, have you?"

Jon shook his head. "Nope. And I even went outside and looked after you called, just in case. I know Drackett was out at the explosion scene this morning."

Derek sat in his chair. "I checked the security log. No record of her scan card being swiped. I'm a little concerned that maybe she was more injured last night than she let on. Maybe something happened and she called for an ambulance or something."

"Let me call the local hospitals, see if she got brought in."

"Okay." Derek nodded at him. "I'm going to go back to the lab, or what's left of it, to see if she's there. Maybe Steve knows something."

The director was outside, walking around the site of last night's fire. He was talking with multiple people. Derek could only imagine the amount of paperwork headache something like this had to cause. He didn't envy Drackett's position, especially not right now.

When he saw Derek's nod, Steve excused himself from the group of people he was consulting with. "Everything okay inside?"

"Is Molly Humphries out here with you?"

"No. I haven't seen her since you took her home last night."

That was not what Derek had been hoping to hear. "She seems to be MIA. I was supposed to pick her up this morning, but she wasn't at her house. No record of her signing in here."

"It's not like Molly to just not show up."

"Jon is checking hospitals. I'm concerned she may have been more injured than she let on."

The director grimaced. "I hope not. Keep me posted. I've got my hands full out here trying to figure out what happened and how to move forward. As a matter of fact, I could really use Molly's input if she shows up." The older man slapped Derek on the shoulder. "*When* she shows up."

Derek nodded, but wasn't convinced. "I'll send her out here when I see her."

By the time he'd made it back inside and to his desk Jon had a report. "Well, good news, or bad, depending on how you want to look at it. She's not at any of the hospitals. I checked any Jane Does, too, just to be thorough."

The itch he'd had at the back of his neck since there'd been no answer at Molly's door was back in full force.

"Something's not right. I just know it." He looked over at Jon. "Am I overreacting?"

"You told Molly you'd pick her up this morning? And she seemed fine when you left?"

Well, no, actually she'd seemed a little upset because— jackass that he was—he'd told her he didn't want to kiss her because she had plaster in her hair.

"She didn't seem injured if that's what you mean."

Jon shook his head. "I've watched her hang on every word you say for the last three years. Watched her eyes follow you all around a room every time you enter it. Feelings which—congratulations to you for being such a good actor and fooling us all—I assumed were one-sided on her part."

Jon was a damned good behavioral analyst, but Derek didn't like to find himself on the other end of Jon's skills. "What's your point, Hatton?"

"Actually, my point is that I agree with you. I don't think you're overreacting. If you told Molly you would be there to pick her up this morning, there is not much that would keep her from being there when that happened if she had a say."

Derek wasn't sure about all that, but he did know Molly was a considerate and kind person. She would've left a note, *something* if she knew she wasn't going to be there for him when she said she would.

Derek wasn't ignoring his gut any longer. Yeah, they

needed to get back out to the house in West Philly, but first Derek was going to make sure Molly was all right. He sat down at his desk.

"What's your plan?" Jon asked.

"I'm going to see what sort of street-camera footage we have on Molly's house. She has a stoplight nearby."

"Give me her address and I'll help look, too."

Accessing camera footage wasn't as easy or as simple as cop shows made it look on TV. Watching it was time-consuming and boring work, often leading to nothing.

But not this time.

If Derek hadn't been watching for it, he wouldn't have seen it since the perps hugged the shadows so well.

"Jon. Look at this."

The traffic light camera provided footage of two men entering the alley behind Molly's condo. Twenty minutes later they left down the same alley, but this time they were carrying someone between them.

The expletives that flew out of Derek's mouth were ugly. Jon's weren't much better.

They watched it again.

"Someone took Molly. Why the hell would someone take Molly?" Jon murmured to no one in particular.

For the second time in twenty-four hours Derek had to completely divorce himself from his feelings. There was no room for panic. There was only room for the task at hand.

Finding the bastards that took Molly and getting her home safely.

Sometimes the toughest part of taking action was when you knew there was no action to take yet. The *why* of someone taking Molly was secondary right now to the *who* and the *where*.

"I'm tasking every available camera in that area to see if we can get an ID or at least a vehicle."

"You take the ones running north and south. I'll start east/west."

Definitely faster this way. Neither of them spoke as they used the computers to find and utilize any cameras near Molly's house. And neither of them gave a damn that they didn't have the necessary prior approval to do so.

If Steve Drackett was pissed at what they were doing, Derek would take the heat. But they were already hours behind Molly's abductors. Derek wasn't going to waste time running outside to get Drackett's written permission.

Every second was precious.

"I've got something. ATM camera." Jon spun in his chair to face Derek. "Same black SUV leaving. Heading west down Monument Street at 5:12 a.m."

Five-twelve? That was barely fifteen minutes after he'd left Molly's house. Derek clenched his fists. As if he hadn't had enough reason to have wished he'd stayed.

Derek concentrated his efforts on the cameras that would pick up the SUV. It was like piecing together a puzzle, figuring out which way the vehicle turned at an intersection, often by process of elimination.

But as the vehicle headed farther out of the city, there were fewer cameras to track it.

"We're going to lose it." Derek's teeth were gritted as he made the statement. "It's heading out of town."

Sure enough, within a few minutes they'd lost the SUV completely. There just weren't enough cameras.

Derek slammed his fist down on his desk.

"Let me see if we can get anything by working with the cameras from different angles or with reflections," Jon told him.

It wasn't as good as getting an actual location where the vehicle had stopped, but it may get them a usable photo of one of the two people who had taken Molly. Better than nothing.

While Jon worked that, Derek went back to footage at Molly's condo. He watched again as the men carried her out, one holding her legs, the other her torso. She seemed to be totally slack, not struggling in any way.

If Derek was working this case objectively, looking at this footage and not knowing it was Molly, he'd say that there was every possibility that the two men were carrying out a dead body.

But Derek refused to even consider that possibility now, even though the stillness of her body frightened him to his core. Damn it, why did it seem as if he was praying for Molly's life to be spared so often over the past twenty-four hours?

"I've got something!" Jon's excitement was palpable. "A clear shot of the driver's face."

Derek rushed over to Jon's computer so he could see. "I don't recognize him at all. You?"

"No, nothing. But let's run him through facial recognition and see if we get a hit."

It was a long shot, but it was the best shot they had. But it also meant more waiting.

"This has to be tied to the lab fire last night," Derek said.

"Yeah, but maybe we were wrong about it having to do with the Chicago bombing case. Maybe it was someone trying to get rid of Molly, and when that didn't work, they took her. There was a lot of evidence in that lab."

Derek had to admit it was possible. "Definitely an angle to consider."

"But it's also a pretty big coincidence after everything that happened in Philly. Unless all the bad guys have gone overboard crazy at once."

"Right now, I'm not ruling anything out. I just want to get Molly back."

"Absolutely." Jon pounded him on the shoulder. "I'm going to look over footage from last night's fire. See if anyone was around."

Derek nodded. "I'm going to look through everything we have from yesterday at the house. If this is all tied together, maybe it could provide us with something."

What it could provide, Derek had no idea. All he knew for certain was that every moment he had nothing was another moment where Molly was in the clutches of some unknown foe.

Using the same method they had earlier, Derek began looking for accessible cameras near yesterday's house in West Philly. The area wasn't nearly as busy, or as wealthy, as the area where Omega HQ and Molly's neighborhood was located, so cameras were more sparse. Most of the ones he could find didn't produce results of any value.

He was about to call it a dead end when an unusual reflection caught his eye in one of the traffic cameras. A black car parked about two blocks from the site. Not an SUV like the one that had taken Molly, but a four-door sedan that looked completely out of place in that neighborhood.

Derek watched as the camera's canted angle showed the perpetrator who had eventually killed himself yesterday walking up to the car. The backseat window rolled down halfway, but Derek couldn't see inside. After a brief conversation, the now-dead man ran away, toward the house where Derek, Jon and Liam would be showing up a few minutes later.

The sedan quickly pulled away and Derek barely caught the most important feature as it sped up the street.

"Jon, get over here and look at this."

"What?"

Derek ran the footage for him and then paused it right at the end, pointing to the license plate of the sedan. A small sticker that made all the difference.

"Secret Service." Jon shook his head as he said it.

"Somebody under Secret Service's protection was meeting with the guy who'd rather kill himself than be taken into custody a few minutes before we got there."

The US Secret Service guarded a lot more than just the president. Their duties included protection of congressmen and senators as well as certain dignitaries. Hundreds of people.

But it was definitely one more link strengthening the theory that someone pretty high in the US Government had some part in the Chicago bombing. They would need to get this info to Drackett as soon as possible.

But it didn't get them any closer to figuring out who took Molly.

As if it could read Derek's thoughts, his computer pinged. Facial recognition had a hit on the picture of the guy from the SUV that had taken her.

Derek printed the findings of the facial recognition program. He and Jon stared at it, both of them trying to figure out the ramifications.

The man they were looking at wasn't important in and of himself. It was who he was a known associate of that drew their attention.

The man worked for Pablo Belisario, a known drug lord from Colombia. Derek tried to wrap his head around that.

What in the hell did a drug lord from Colombia want with Molly?

"Belisario? Is someone in Omega actively investigating him?" Derek asked.

Jon pulled up some info on his computer. "Not that's

listed. I guess someone could be doing undercover work. But what would that have to do with Molly?"

Derek shook his head. "I have no idea." Anything undercover wouldn't be fielded through the Critical Response Division offices. Omega had its own main office in Washington, DC, for undercover ops, and they had their own labs. "I felt sure whoever had taken her was going to be tied into the terrorist attack in some way. But Belisario? He's too chump change for something the size of Chicago."

Belisario wasn't a terrorist. But he was known for his ruthlessness and violence. The thought of Molly in his hands—for whatever unknown reason—was sickening. Something had to be done.

Right damn now.

"We need to run everything we can about Belisario immediately."

Derek and Jon spent the rest of the afternoon tracking down every piece of information they could about Pablo Belisario. Derek found Liam Goetz, knowing the other agent had some background in Vice.

"Belisario is continually on the DEA watch list," Liam told him. "He's become a bigger player over the last year. But I have no idea what he would have to do with Molly."

"Neither do I," Derek told him. "I've run all the cases that were listed in the system that the lab was currently processing. Nothing to do with drugs or Belisario."

"Let me call in a few favors with some old contacts in the DEA. See what the current word is about it."

"Thanks, Liam. I don't know what the hell is going on, but I know we've got to get Molly back."

Liam picked up the phone right then. "As soon as possible. Because Belisario is one mean bastard. I can't stand the thought of sweet Molly in his hands."

Neither could Derek.

Within a few hours—long, agonizing hours for Derek—they had some answers. Belisario was under surveillance by local Colombians the DEA had carefully hired. They reported back daily to the DEA on Belisario's movements. Over the past twenty-four hours there had been no word of Belisario leaving his well-fortified home. But there had been a report of a woman being dragged into the house this afternoon, unable to walk on her own.

A white woman with long brown hair.

Chapter Eight

As soon as he heard the description of the woman, Derek was on his feet. He had no doubt this was Molly. It had to be.

"Listen, man." Liam put a hand on his shoulder. "Evidently women being dragged into Belisario's house is not an uncommon thing. This may not even be Molly."

"A white woman with long brown hair just a few hours after Molly was taken by one of his known associates? It has to be her." It was time to do something. He started walking down the hall.

"Where are you going?" Jon called after him.

Derek didn't even slow down. "Drackett's office. We all know that's Molly."

He didn't wait to see if the other two men were coming with him. He didn't expect them to. Just like Derek wasn't going to the director's office to get his permission. He was going to tell him because he respected Drackett and his boss deserved to know why he would be MIA for the next unknown number of hours or days.

However long it took to get Molly out of the hands of a sadistic drug lord.

Derek knocked once on Drackett's door as he was opening it. The director didn't seem too surprised to see him.

Derek, on the other hand, was a little surprised to find Jon and Liam had followed him into Drackett's office.

"I've already been apprised of the situation," Steve told them without any formal greeting.

Derek should've known Drackett would be aware of what was going on, even with the chaos from last night's fire to deal with. That's why he was the director.

"DEA contacts put a Caucasian woman with long brown hair being forcefully taken into Belisario's estate a couple hours ago," Derek reported.

"Knowing we wouldn't be able to confirm if that was Molly or not—"

"Steve—" Derek didn't need confirmation. He was moving regardless of whether they were 100 percent sure.

Steve held up his hand and started over. "Knowing we wouldn't be able to confirm if the woman was Molly, I immediately tasked a satellite to give us footage of his property as soon as I got word of that."

This was why Steve Drackett was the director of one of the most important law enforcement agencies in the country. The man made decisions and didn't waste time. Derek was tempted to lean over the desk and kiss him.

"Don't get too excited," Drackett told them. "I was still unable to confirm it was her. But I was able to positively confirm that this man was present on the premises this afternoon."

He slid a picture across his desk.

"That's Santiago. He's the one that was at Molly's condo last night. We had positive ID on him."

Drackett nodded. "I know. Which is why I agree that Molly is the woman spotted by the DEA contact being taken into the estate."

Derek had been prepared to move at much less confirmation than this. "I'm going down there."

Drackett stood and looked Derek directly in the eye. "We have zero jurisdiction down there."

"I don't care." Derek knew where Molly was and he was going to get her out. Or die trying.

"No agency of the US Government can send in a team into a situation like this. Not if we don't know for sure who the woman is or why she's there," Jon chimed in.

"I don't care," Derek repeated, nodding at Jon. He knew whatever he was going to do was going to be unofficial. He'd be on his own. Drackett couldn't have any official knowledge of it.

He turned back to Steve. "I just came in here to tell you I was going to need a couple of personal days off. Not sure exactly how long."

Steve looked at him for a long moment. Then finally nodded.

"Oh man, Steve, and I forgot to tell you, I need a few days off, too," Jon said.

Surprised, Derek looked over at Jon. Derek would've never asked this of his friend—it was potentially both career- and life-threatening. But he needed all the help he could get.

Jon nodded at him and shrugged.

"Seriously, you guys? This is so stupid." Liam rolled his eyes and turned and walked toward the office door. "Which is why I just remembered I need time off, too, Drackett. I think I put in the paperwork for it last week, but you probably lost it."

When Derek turned to look at him, Liam grinned and winked. For the first time since he realized Molly was missing the tightness in Derek's chest loosened just the slightest bit. There were no other people Derek would rather have at his back in a situation like this than Liam and Jon.

The director sat back down behind his desk. "Gentlemen, if you don't mind I have a lot to do here with last night's fire fiasco. For the life of me I can't even remember what you came in here to tell me besides to remind me of your time off which was approved over two weeks ago."

"Thanks, Steve." Those two words didn't say nearly enough.

"Listen, you guys do me a favor, okay?" Drackett continued as they turned to leave. "The oversight committee is pretty concerned about security here at the building after last night's episode. Jon, since you're a pilot, I need you to relocate one of the Omega planes before you officially go on vacation, okay? Just go to any of the approved airfields in North or South America. Just so I can keep my superiors happy. And you should probably clear out some of the weapons lockers for the same reason. Security."

"Steve—" Jon started.

Everybody knew that if all this went bad Drackett would have a hard time explaining things. But providing them with an unofficial plane and weapons was probably making the difference between success and failure.

"Why are you guys still here? I don't have time for chatting today. Enjoy your vacation."

Derek looked at Liam and Jon. They planned on it.

DEREK KNOCKED ON *her door. She'd been watching* The Avengers *for the umpteenth time and had honestly thought it was one of her neighbors at the condo. Who else would be knocking at her door at eleven at night on a Friday? When she peeped through and saw it was Derek she'd been so surprised she'd just opened the door in her pajama shorts and oversize Georgia Tech sweatshirt.*

For the first time since she'd known him, which had been for over a year, the gorgeous agent looked indecisive.

"Derek, um, hi. Are you okay?"

He just stood there in her doorway, looking slightly rumpled and all the more sexy because of it.

"Is there an emergency at work?" she asked him.

"No. Nothing to do with work."

His deep voice sent heat to places Molly didn't think about very often.

"Oh, okay." She wasn't sure what to do or say, which wasn't unusual for her. But usually Derek knew what to say. Although evidently not tonight. "Are you okay?"

"I told myself not to stop by. Then I decided I would because I thought you wouldn't be home."

That didn't make any sense to her. Why would he come by if he thought she wouldn't be home?

"Oh, okay." And now she sounded like a parrot. "Um, do you want to come in?"

"I probably shouldn't." But he took the slightest unsteady step forward.

And then it hit her. "Oh my gosh, Derek. Are you drunk?"

He cocked his head sideways and smiled, a boyish grin completely at odds with Derek's size and darker features. "I might be just a wee bit tipsy."

Molly's insides completely melted.

Derek Waterman: superagent. Strong, tough and completely cool under pressure was standing right in front of her, a wee bit tipsy.

She'd seen him in the lab multiple times over the past few months and could admit she had a crush on him, but she never dreamed he'd show up at her house. Looking closer at him she could see the tension around his eyes, the slightly haggard look on his face.

Whatever had led to the wee *bit tipsy had been fueled by something much darker and harder. Decisions he'd had to make as an agent. Or violent and terrible things he'd seen. Molly experienced some of that secondhand in the lab, but never up close like Derek did on a daily basis.*

Derek Waterman needed a friend. She didn't know why he'd come to her, but she was more than willing to be a friend to someone in need. Especially someone who had dedicated his life to helping others.

He looked a little surprised when she grabbed his hand and pulled him the rest of the way inside. "You didn't drive, right?"

He looked affronted. "Of course not. The guys and I were at a bar just a few blocks from here." He rubbed his eyes with his hand. "It was a bad day today."

The demons in his eyes were evident. "I'm sorry." She couldn't help herself; she reached up and touched his cheek. "You can stay here as long as you want."

He closed his eyes and leaned his cheek into her hand, not saying anything.

"Do you want me to make some coffee?" she said softly. "I was just watching a movie. We could do that if you want. Or just talk."

Derek opened his eyes and looked at her slowly from head to toe.

Molly wished she was wearing a little bit of makeup. And wasn't in her pajamas. But the look in his eyes said he didn't care. She shivered.

He reached out and touched the hair that had fallen over her shoulders.

"No braid," he said, taking a step closer. "No lab coat."

Molly's laugh was rueful. "Yeah, contrary to popular opinion, neither are permanent fixtures on my body."

"This was how I knew you'd look—sweet." He took another step closer, still holding her hair. Molly's breath hitched as he hooked his finger in the loose collar of the sweatshirt under her hair and slid it until it fell completely off one shoulder. He slowly moved her hair to the other side so her neck and shoulder were exposed.

She was very aware that she had nothing on under that sweatshirt. He had to be, too. She knew that she should stop this. That he'd had too much to drink. That he needed a friend.

But watching him transfixed by her bare skin, Molly could no more stop this than she could stop breathing.

But she did stop breathing when she felt his lips against her collarbone, moving with featherlike kisses down the length of her shoulder.

"Derek..." His name came out in a breathy whisper.

"So soft. So gentle. I knew you would be." His voice was right next to her ear, then his lips moved down to her neck and throat.

When Molly's knees threatened to buckle, he wrapped an arm around her waist and backed her up against the hallway wall. His mouth came down in a painless bite right where her shoulder met her neck. Molly moaned, wrapping her arms around his neck and pulling him closer.

"Where's your bedroom?"

She waved her arm in the general direction of the stairway before bringing it back to his neck and pulling his face down to hers, his mouth to her own.

He never stopped kissing her as he slid an arm under her knees and picked her up, not even breathing any harder after carrying her up the stairs. He set her down next to her bed and pulled her sweatshirt over her head and pulled the shorts completely off her body.

Molly was very aware that she was completely naked while he was still fully dressed. She reached for his shirt, but he stopped her, grabbing her wrists gently and holding her arms out to the side.

"No. Let me look at you." He trailed a finger from her cheek, down her throat and over both breasts. "You're so damn beautiful, Molly. So beautiful."

She reached for him again, and this time he didn't stop her, kissing her again after she unbuttoned his shirt and pushed it from his shoulders. He made short work of his pants and they fell into bed together.

Molly tried to take a moment of sanity, to make sure this was what Derek was looking for. That it wasn't just the drinks he'd had that had led them to this moment. She flipped her weight around so that he was lying on his back on the bed and she was kneeling over him.

"Derek, maybe we should wait. Make sure that this is what you really want."

He froze for just a moment, silent, looking up at her. Molly was sure he had come to his senses, that he realized this wasn't what he was looking for, that he was just drunk. Then he reached up and gently touched a strand of her hair from the roots all the way down to the tips where it rested on his chest.

Without saying a word he flipped her back over, grabbing her leg and hooking it over his hip. Molly gasped as she could feel every inch of both their naked bodies against each other.

"Does it feel like you aren't what I really want?"

Molly started to answer, but someone ripped her violently out of the bed and threw her on the floor. She looked around blinking, trying to get her bearings.

This wasn't her condo. She wasn't with Derek, she had been dreaming. Remembering.

Her reality was a room with no window and a filthy cot, and standing over her were the two men who had taken her from her home.

Chapter Nine

The memory of her wonderful night with Derek made waking to this reality that much more terrifying. They laughed as she scampered back until she hit a dirt wall.

Where was she? Who were these men? Why had they taken her? What did they want?

Molly racked her still-fuzzy brain. They'd taken her on a plane somewhere, right? She didn't know for sure, but the plane had been the last mode of transportation she'd seen.

She was still in the yoga pants and T-shirt she'd put on after her shower at home, however many hours ago. Her bra and underwear were still in place, which made her feel better.

Surely they wouldn't have violated her unconscious body and then bothered to completely redress her.

The two men were speaking Spanish with a little English thrown in, and both had dark enough hair and skin to be from Mexico or South America. But narrowing it down to a continent didn't get any of Molly's questions answered.

She definitely had been drugged. Not only did she remember the pinpricks, she could still feel the aftereffects: mushy head, thirsty, tongue feeling swollen. Of course her whole face felt swollen from where Jerk #2 had hit her after she'd run.

"What do you want with me?"

Molly's voice sounded strange, distant, to her own ears, much lower than her normal pitch. A side effect of the drug, no doubt. What had it been? Rohypnol? Ketamine? GHB? Molly had worked dozens of cases in the lab over the years dealing with these common date-rape drugs. She tried to remember specific ramifications of each, but couldn't seem to force her brain to do it.

And then the men were coming toward her and she totally forgot about the drugs. They didn't answer her question about what they wanted with her, just grabbed her under her armpits and dragged her through the door.

Not wanting to get punched again, Molly didn't try to run or yell. Walking without falling over was difficult enough. She'd never be able to escape them, especially with one flanked on either side. Right now she just needed to focus. To gather as many details as possible about what was going on. To try to come up with a plan.

They went down a short hallway before a door opened to the outside. Glancing over her shoulder, Molly realized she'd been held in some sort of servant's quarters or something. They were now crossing under an extended portico to a much larger house. A mansion. She could see men with large guns guarding it.

Despite the fact that the sun was going down, it was still warm. They must have traveled south. Maybe they really were in Mexico or South America. Everyone she had seen so far looked to be Hispanic.

Hysteria swamped her at the thought of being in a completely foreign country, having no idea where or with whom, but she tamped it down. Panic wasn't going to get her anywhere.

And she was afraid panic was going to be her only option in a little while anyway. Might as well save it.

They took her through the back door into the house.

It was beautiful inside, if a touch melodramatic with marble floors and heavy drapery hanging in the windows. Paintings of all different types decorated the walls while vases and sculptures lined the tables in the vast foyer. It was like some weirdly interpreted copy of Tara from *Gone with the Wind*.

The two men brought her into the very formal living room with furniture so fancy it would've made Molly afraid to sit on it even in normal circumstances. She stopped walking and was dragged from the doorway to the middle of the room. A man with black hair combed back and dressed in light linen pants and a dark shirt rose from one of the large leather wingback chairs.

"So you're finally awake, Ms. Humphries. It took much longer than I thought. My name is Pablo Belisario. This is my home."

He spoke in English, but his accent was thick. Although his name sounded vaguely familiar, Molly still didn't know who this man was or what he wanted with her.

He continued, "It seems my men gave you too much of the drug when they first took you. You've been unconscious for over twelve hours." Molly fought not to cringe as he walked around her in a circle. "You're quite petite, the second dose they gave could've been fatal."

He glared at the men holding her. "Fortunately for your sake—and for theirs—it was not."

What was she supposed to say to this? Thank you? She finally decided silence was probably better.

"But your lack of consciousness for so long has caused a delay in answers I need right away." His glare turned from the men to her.

"I'm sorry. I'm not sure what you are talking about. Answers about what?" Maybe it was still the drugs making her fuzzy, but Molly had absolutely no idea what

Belisario was referring to. "I think maybe you have the wrong person."

His sigh was impatient. "No, Ms. Humphries. We very definitely have the right person. I just need to know what you found out in the lab yesterday before it was destroyed. And exactly who you told about it."

Molly shook her head, trying to clear cobwebs. She would be confused even if she didn't have Rohypnol or whatever in her system. Belisario had brought her here to ask her about the lab fire?

"There are—*were*—a lot of items in the lab. Could you tell me, um, what sort of business you're in?"

Belisario's eyes narrowed. "I'm a little disappointed you don't know who I am already."

Molly backtracked. The last thing she wanted to do was injure this man's pride in any way. "Well, I'm a geek, in a lab all the time. I don't get out much." Sadly, that was true. "I probably wouldn't know ninety percent of celebrities if I saw them on the street."

"You've already become acquainted with one of my best sellers. It's what has made you sleep so long. But most of my empire has been built on cocaine."

The true identity of the man suddenly clicked into place. He had told her who he was, but she hadn't made the connection. He was Pablo Belisario, head of one of the largest drug manufacturing and dealing operations in South America. She really only knew about him because of consulting with the DEA a couple years ago.

Molly sucked in a breath as she now understood how much danger she was really in. Belisario's reputation was brutal. Lethal.

"Ah, I see you now have figured out who I am." His smile made Molly's skin crawl. "I must admit that makes me happy."

He stepped closer, more focused on her than he had been just a few minutes before. "You are much prettier than I thought you would be." He touched her cheek.

Molly knew with absolute certainty that the center of this man's attention was a very bad place to be.

"Mr. Belisario, yes, your reputation is very well-known." Molly knew she had to get his attention off her personally, although she didn't know where to direct it. She'd never handled anything in the lab having to do with him. "But I'm sure nothing in the lab had any incriminating evidence about you."

"No, I'm not worried about my operations. I have a partner, who shall remain...unmentioned. He needs to know what you know."

That really didn't narrow it down for Molly. "Mr. Belisario, I was working on dozens of cases in the lab yesterday, and honestly, I don't remember many details about any of them."

He shrugged, giving an exaggerated sigh. "You know, I tried to make that exact point to my partner. I told him to just leave it alone. But he is prone toward the melodramatic."

Almost as if he couldn't stop touching her, he reached over and grasped her chin in his hand, turning her head side to side, as if he was inspecting her. "Yesterday was quite the bad day for him. Seems like evidence linking him to...certain crimes was obtained, despite his attempts to keep that from happening."

Despite herself, Molly pulled her head away and Belisario's eyes narrowed.

"He tried to destroy all evidence at the scene first," Belisario continued. "But evidently a few key pieces were still recovered by your Omega agents. So then he planted a bomb to destroy the entire lab."

Oh, no. All of this was about the evidence that Derek had brought in yesterday. Concerning the Chicago bombing.

He touched her cheek again and Molly forced herself to hold still. "You, my dear, were supposed to have died in the fire, in case you knew anything. But you somehow made it out.

"Once we found out you had survived the explosion, he needed you questioned. And that couldn't take place on US soil, so he asked me to bring you here. He needs to know what you found yesterday in the lab and who you told."

"I don't know anything—"

His backhand nearly knocked her to the floor. If his henchmen hadn't been on either side of her, she would've fallen. Molly tasted blood in her mouth, the pain compounded by the bruise she already had on her face.

"You see, Ms. Humphries, I don't have time for responses like 'I don't know anything.'" He shook his head almost apologetically. "So I'm going to need you to give me specific information about what was in the lab."

He nodded briefly to the henchman on the left. Before Molly even knew what to expect, his fist came piling into her midsection.

Molly doubled over as pain stole her breath in a way she didn't even know was possible. She tried to sob, but no sound or air came out. Almost immediately the other henchman pulled her back upright by her hair.

"Let's be honest with one another." Belisario's tone was almost bored. "You are small, delicate. A scientist. You're not the type who will be able to bounce back quickly from severe questioning. From torture." He grabbed her jaw again and squeezed it painfully. She felt tears stream down her face. "I need specific details, Ms. Humphries."

"I—I…" Molly tried to get her thoughts together, to get

her breathing under control now that her airways seemed to be working. "The agents brought in something from a fire, a building that had burned down earlier in the day."

He released her face. "Yes. Very good. Continue. Which agents brought it in?"

Molly didn't care if they hit her again. She wasn't giving this psychopath Derek's or any other agents' names. She thought fast. "Steve Rogers was the main agent. I can't remember the other guy."

She felt a cruel yank on her hair. "Details, Ms. Humphries."

"He's new, so I'm not sure. I think his name is Bruce something. Banner, maybe." She prayed none of the men were Marvel comic or *The Avenger* fans, since she was basically just listing characters now.

"And?"

"I didn't have a chance to get to any of what they brought in. The lab was backed up. I was planning to work all night. I had stepped out to get a bite to eat, that's why I wasn't in the lab when the explosion happened." That was the truth.

Belisario nodded at the man standing behind her holding her hair. He brought her arm behind her back in a cruel twist that had Molly crying out.

"Just the slightest pressure from Henrico and your arm will break in quite a nasty way. So make sure you answer completely—did you talk to anyone about what was brought in by the agents? Does anyone know anything that could come back to haunt my partner?"

"Not from me, not from our lab. Everything was destroyed. I promise. If there was anything more to tell you I would." Molly could feel her arm being inched up behind her back. Henrico was definitely looking forward to doing damage.

Belisario looked at her for a long moment, then thankfully shook his head at Henrico. He let her go and threw her away from him, anger in his eyes when she glanced at him, rubbing her aching shoulder.

"You see? Not so difficult when you provide the right details," Belisario said. "And I believe you, because I'm sure you can imagine what will happen to you if I discover any part of this is a lie."

Molly shuddered and Belisario laughed.

He ran a finger down her cheek again and Molly blanched before she could help it. This earned her a slap. "I'm supposed to kill you now, that's what my partner wants, in case you talk to anyone. But like I said, he can be a bit overdramatic. There's no need to kill you yet. I'm sure I can find other uses for you."

His finger trailed down her shoulder and Molly looked away.

"Plus, we want to check all those details you gave us. Make sure they were true. And if even one small part isn't, then we'll start this whole questioning process again."

Molly struggled not to vomit right then. It wouldn't take long for whoever Belisario's partner was to figure out that the names she'd given were fake, even if everything else was true.

A phone rang in Belisario's pocket and he moved away from her. "I have business to attend to now. But we'll talk again soon." He turned to his men. "Take her back."

It was dark outside as they returned her to her room.

"I'm sure the boss will let us have our turn with her after he's done," Henrico said to the other guy.

Molly choked back a sob. She was hungry, thirsty, tired and ached all over. The thought of these men touching her was almost more than she could handle. When they opened the door to her room, Henrico reached down and squeezed her buttocks.

Molly elbowed him in the stomach and jerked away, making the other henchman laugh.

Enraged, Henrico threw her down on the floor. He kicked her with one booted foot in the thigh. Molly cried out in pain and scampered backward to try to get out of his reach. He grabbed her by the front of her shirt and brought her torso off the ground.

"And when the boss lets me have you, you will beg me for death." He backhanded her across the face and threw her down.

Although that hit wasn't as hard as the others, it was too much for Molly. She just let the blackness consume her.

Chapter Ten

This was not how Derek liked to go into a situation: totally blind. But he didn't have much choice. He and Liam poured over all of the intel they could get their hands on about Belisario's home—which was more like a compound—as Jon flew them down to Colombia.

Derek liked to have the tactical advantage in all professional situations. He even liked having it in personal ones. But he had to admit there was no real tactical advantage for them here.

"Covert entry is pretty much our only option and our only advantage," he said to Liam. "If we have to go in guns blazing, our chance of success is pretty darn low. We just don't have the manpower needed to take down Belisario in his own nest."

"Quiet, it is." Liam was leaning with his head back against his seat, eyes closed, but Derek knew the other man was aware of everything going on around him. "My kung fu is strong."

Using night as their cover, Derek and Liam would be parachuting out to land closer to Belisario's property. It was risky, but it would get them there much faster. Derek was willing to risk just about anything to get them there faster.

Every additional minute it took them to get there was

a minute Molly was left alone in heaven knew what type of situation.

Jon would have to land the plane almost ten miles from the property in order not to be seen. It was the only place in the dense rain forest with enough clearing for a landing strip. He would have the plane ready for takeoff upon Derek and Liam's return with Molly, backup firearms ready in case they were coming in hot.

Although hostage rescue was Liam's specialty and jumping out of planes into questionable situations was his particular forte, it had been years since Derek had done this sort of thing.

"You'll do fine. It's just like 'Stan, only greener." Derek found Liam looking over at him. They'd both been in Special Forces in Afghanistan for multiple tours. Both knew what it was to take a life, to make the hard call, to do things that left scars on the soul. Even though Derek didn't use that training any more in his day-to-day duties, his time there had made him into the man he was.

As Special Forces, both he and Liam knew how to infiltrate silently and deadly. That's what they'd be doing here. Because if they got caught, there wouldn't be anyone coming to help them. Omega would not be able to acknowledge Derek's mission in any way. The official word would be that they had acted on their own.

"Besides, I know how to speak Spanish, so that gives us an advantage," Liam said.

Derek studied Liam. He'd known the other man for a lot of years and didn't know he spoke Spanish. "You do?"

Liam shrugged. "The important stuff. *Hola hermosa bebé, creo que deberíamos pasar la noche juntos.*"

Derek was pretty sure Liam had just called him pretty and asked him if he wanted to spend the night. Derek rolled his eyes. Knowing Liam, he wouldn't be surprised if that was the only Spanish the other man knew at all.

Of course, Derek also wouldn't be surprised to find out that the man spoke it fluently. You just never knew with Liam.

"Thanks, Liam," Derek said.

"Thanks for calling you pretty?" Liam winked at him.

"For doing this. I know the risks. I know you do, too." Their lives, their careers. Everything. Without Jon and Liam, Derek's chances of getting Molly out alive would be practically zero.

The odds with them weren't terribly higher either, but at least they had a chance.

Liam was serious now, a rare occurrence. "I assumed Molly was irrelevant to you. I think we all did."

Derek stared at the other man for a long minute. "No, she's never been irrelevant to me. The opposite." He hardly had words for what Molly was to him. "She's my light. Pure and lovely and…" Derek shrugged. He wasn't good with words.

"She's everything you're afraid of dragging down into your dark and dirty world. Extinguishing the light." Liam finished for him. "So you've stayed away. Made everyone—including her—think you don't care."

Derek nodded. All of that was exactly right.

"Good thing I didn't ask her out like I considered. I had grand dreams of being the one to help her get over the stupid jerk who didn't seem to appreciate what was right in front of him." And just like that Liam's seriousness was gone. "Would've sucked to have my nose broken when you punched me in the face."

To be honest Derek wasn't sure what he would've done if Molly had gone out with someone else. Especially a friend.

Liam was back to serious. "You'd do the same for me,

if I needed help, Derek. And all of us would do anything for sweet Molly."

"Ten minutes till we're in the drop zone," Jon called back from the cockpit of the small plane.

"Roger that," Derek responded. He turned to Liam. "Any questions about our plan?"

"Rendezvous with each other on the ground. Get into the estate at the weak spot in the wall near the northeast corner. Find our girl and get her out. All undetected."

That was the plan. Now all they had to do was pull it off.

MOLLY DIDN'T PARTICULARLY like autopsies. She did have a degree in forensic pathology, was a certified medical examiner, so not liking autopsies was probably a little odd. But she had never been able to distance herself from the body on her table, and sympathized about what had happened to them.

And since she worked at Omega, most autopsies she performed were often pretty gruesome deaths. Most of the time Molly was able to foster out the autopsies to one of the other two pathologists employed by the lab; neither ever seemed to mind.

But sometimes, like now, it had to be Molly. It was late in the evening, everyone else had gone home. The two bodies in the morgue were Omega agents who had been killed in a hostage rescue situation. She knew them. Not as well as she knew some of the other agents, but enough that what she was doing—removing bullets that would later be used in the case against the criminals who did this—was harder. But she wanted to get it done as soon as possible so the bodies could be released to the grieving families.

She felt eyes on her from across the room, and looked up. There was Derek standing silently watching her.

It had been two years since that night he'd shown up

at her house. The night she thought about all the time. The night that had haunted her dreams and caused her to wake up aching for Derek. The night that had changed everything for her.

The night the two of them had never once spoken about.

When she'd awakened the next morning—after multiple bouts of lovemaking, since every time she'd even slid away from him, even when he'd been sleeping, he'd pulled her back to him and tucked her against him—he'd been gone.

Molly thought maybe he'd been too drunk to remember what had happened. But medically she knew that was highly unlikely. If Derek had been sober enough to...ahem, perform...that many times, then he hadn't been inebriated to the point of blocking the night out of his subconscious.

Then she had feared even worse: that she'd just been a one-night stand, a conquest Derek would boast about to his friends. The thought had made her ill. But there had been nothing that anyone had ever said or did—no knowing glances or sideways winks—that had insinuated that Derek had spoken to anyone about it. Since that night, Derek himself had been polite, respectful.

Distant.

He never touched her. Not even casually like he had before. He was very deliberate in the not touching her, although Molly didn't think anyone else noticed. It wasn't as if they'd walked around arm in arm before that night. But now, nothing.

And Molly, pansy that she was, had developed some sort of stutter anytime he was near. She'd always been a little awkward around him, but after that night she was a complete moron. Everyone assumed that she was just a socially awkward scientist who got tongued-tied around a super-sexy, mega-hot agent she had a crush on. Which was true.

No one suspected her body remembered every single touch and lick and nibble from their night together causing her to go into overdrive every time Derek was around. Which was also true.

Derek did an excellent job of being distant and making sure no one suspected what had happened.

But every once in a while, Molly would catch him watching her with a look in his eyes that melted everything inside her. There was only one word for it.

Heat.

He was quick to blank his face, to school his expression back into its blasted neutrality as soon as he realized she'd seen him. He was so good at it that soon Molly would wonder if she had seen the heat at all.

But now, looking at him across the small morgue attached to the lab, she could see the heat. He didn't do a thing to hide it. She took off her gloves and laid them on the nearby table. He walked over to her without taking his eyes off her face.

And enfolded her in his arms.

She could feel his face buried in her neck, his arms crossing low across her waist and hips. His big body was almost doubled around hers, he had her so close. Molly extracted her arms, trapped between their bodies, so she could wrap them around Derek.

The two dead men had been his colleagues, his friends. As hard as it was for her to have those bodies on the table, it had to be much worse for Derek.

She stroked her hands up and down his back saying nothing. Neither of them said anything. Derek didn't know how to ask for comfort now, for a gentle touch, any more than he'd known how to ask for it when he showed up at her condo two years ago. But that didn't mean he didn't need it.

And Molly would give it, would always give it if it was in her power to do so.

But her leg hurt so badly. And her face.

She moaned. No, pain wasn't part of the memory. There had been no pain in the long minutes where she'd held him before he had gently disengaged himself, kissed her on the forehead, and walked out as silently as he had arrived.

Oh no, she was dreaming again. And was about to wake up to the living nightmare surrounding her. She didn't want that. She wanted to stay here in Derek's arms where she was safe.

"Molly." His finger stroked down her cheek. She felt so secure here. Like nothing could ever hurt her again.

"Molly." The voice was firmer now. She knew she was waking up because everything hurt and Derek hadn't talked to her, he'd been silent.

Well, if she was waking up, she was going to get a kiss in first. She'd always wished she'd kissed him that day in the lab. She drove her hands through his hair and pulled him down to her, not giving him any choice. She kissed him.

And, ah, it felt so good. So real. She so should've kissed him that day. She felt his fingers slip into her hair and pull her closer before moving away. She felt cold without him.

"Molly, sweetheart, I need you to wake up. We've got to get out of here."

She decided not to fight it anymore. She had to wake up and try to find a way out of this. But she wanted to stay in the dream with Derek. "Don't leave me," she whispered to her dream.

"I won't, honey. I promise. But I need you to wake up."

Molly reluctantly opened her eyes to find herself looking in Derek's blue ones, her fingers threaded in his hair.

Chapter Eleven

Molly was alive.

When he'd first seen her lying on the floor at such an awkward angle, Derek had feared he'd been too late. But then she'd moved just the slightest bit and relief crashed through him.

He rushed over to her, cringing as he saw the bruises covering her face, picked her up and laid her on the small cot. She wasn't dead, but that didn't mean she was going to be able to assist them in getting her out of here.

Time was of the essence. The man who had been guarding her door wouldn't be bothering anyone, but all it would take was one person coming to check on Molly and all hell would break loose.

"Molly." He stroked a gentle finger down her damaged cheek. She moved just slightly.

And then she smiled the sweetest smile, cuddling her face down into his hand. Whatever she was dreaming about, it definitely wasn't bad. That reassured him somewhat; better than terror controlling her dreams.

"Molly," he said more firmly. Her smile had faded, but she still hadn't awakened. She could have a head injury or have been drugged.

Then she'd done the damnedest thing: wrapped her hands in his hair and pulled him down to kiss her.

He'd kissed her back before he could even think about it. It was all he'd wanted to do anyway. But sanity soon resumed. No matter how much he wanted to kiss her, this wasn't the time. They had to go.

"Molly, sweetheart, I need you to wake up. We've got to get out of here."

She'd begun to fret and held on to him tighter. "Don't leave me," she whispered.

Derek was so thankful to hear her voice, now she just needed to open her eyes. "I won't, honey. I promise. But I need you to wake up."

And she did.

He watched a plethora of emotions slide over her face: fear, confusion, relief, joy, embarrassment. Her hands dropped out of his hair.

"Derek?"

He smiled at her.

"How did you find me?" she continued.

He framed her face with the gentlest touch he could. "A combination of people committed to finding you and a couple of lucky breaks."

Tears welled in her eyes. "I thought they were going to kill me."

Derek wanted to know why; wanted to know all the details she could tell them about why Belisario had taken her. But not now.

"We've got to go. Every second we spend here is stolen. Liam will cover us as best as he can, but he can't take out all of Belisario's men." Not that his friend wouldn't try if he had to. "Can you walk?"

They'd work on walking first. Hopefully she could run, too. He helped her sit up on the cot, noticing every wince. But she didn't stop or hesitate as he got her up onto her feet.

But she swayed and would've fallen if Derek didn't have

an arm around her. He needed to know exactly what type of injuries they were dealing with. And Molly seemed to have a hard time staying awake. Head trauma?

"Molls, I need you to focus. Can you tell me the worst of your injuries? Do I need to carry you?"

It would make things harder, but Derek was prepared to do it. And despite the kiss that seemed to have rooted from a sweet dream, Derek had to face the very real possibility that Molly had been raped while they'd had her here.

He could see Molly try to gather herself, to concentrate. "My left leg is in a lot of pain—it was kicked—but I don't think it's broken. I was drugged. Rohypnol, I think, or something similar. They gave me too much which is why I keep sleeping."

It was also probably helping to keep the pain under control, or at least make her not focus on it, so the drug wasn't totally a bad thing. But too much still in her system so many hours later was definitely a concern. At least it wasn't a concussion.

And the question he didn't want to ask. "Sweetheart, it's better for me to know now rather than when we're out in the middle of the jungle on the way to the plane—did they…" He couldn't get the word out. "Were you sexually assaulted?"

"No. But it was part of their plan, I know." Her huge brown eyes were laced with terror. "But you got here in time."

Derek closed his eyes. Yes, he was thankful. But they weren't out of the woods yet. Literally or figuratively.

A low whisper came through the headpiece that was attached to his radio. "You got her?"

"Affirmative."

"Can she travel?"

"Affirmative."

Derek heard Liam's short sigh of relief. "Then quit making out or whatever you're doing and get going toward the wall."

"Roger that. Leaving in just a moment."

Very few of Belisario's men were up and around. It was the middle of the night and they had no reason to believe anyone even knew Molly was there, much less expect any sort of rescue attempt.

Their mistake.

Derek knelt down and put a pair of tennis shoes that he'd brought on Molly's feet, since hers were bare. He brought clothes, too, but she was wearing relatively decent clothing, dark yoga pants and a T-shirt, so they weren't needed. Derek wrapped an arm around her and began hustling her toward the door.

"Once we're outside, stay as close as you can to the shadows. This whole place is surrounded by a wall with barbed fencing on top, but there's one place that has an opening we can fit through. We have to cross to the other side of the estate. Liam is covering us and will meet us there."

She nodded and he brought her through the door, deliberately keeping his body between her and the guard who was lying dead outside it. They walked quickly and silently through the dark hallway before Derek cracked the larger outside door, wincing as it made a small sound which seemed to echo in the darkness. Since opening the door slowly seemed to be causing more noise, he jerked it open quickly.

Derek wasted no time pulling Molly through the doorway and outside, shutting the door quickly behind them. It still made a noise, but an open door would be a sure giveaway that something was amiss.

Outside was even more dangerous because there could

be roving guards, or even someone who just came outside to have a cigarette, who could happen upon them and send this entire operation straight to hell. Knowing Liam was out there with his sniper rifle gave them a certain measure of safety. But if he had to use it, things would be going to pot quick, the sound would notify everyone of their presence.

Molly was doing her best to stay with him. To get low when he did, and stick to the shadows. He could tell her leg was hurting her from how she limped. Her shoulders seemed stiff, as if she couldn't get a full range of motion without pain. And one eye was almost swollen shut.

But she didn't complain, not a peep, even when he'd had to throw her to the ground—hard—when a guard had appeared suddenly from behind a nearby building.

They made it to the rendezvous point at the wall, but Liam wasn't there yet. Derek began giving Molly a boost up.

"What about Liam?" she asked.

"He'll be here."

She still looked concerned.

"Baby, hostage rescue is what Liam does. Hell, he thrives on this sort of thing. He'll be here. We've got to make our way through the fence."

Derek was helping Molly through the hole in the fence when from his higher vantage point he saw Liam. But he was running rather than keeping to the shadows. Derek knew that wasn't good, even though no alarm had been raised yet. He urged Molly through faster, and helped her down the other side of the wall.

"What?" she asked him, after seeing his face.

"Liam."

She paled. "Is he hurt?"

"No, but he's running. That's not good."

Out in the thick underbrush of Colombia's rain forest, Derek started moving with Molly. Liam would catch up with them soon enough. They had ten miles to go to get to the plane. Alone, Derek could probably make it in about two hours, given this terrain. But with Molly's condition, it would probably be at least three times that.

They were out of Belisario's estate, but the danger was far from over.

Derek knew Molly needed food and drink, both to give her energy for the journey ahead of them and to continue helping flush the drugs out of her system. He stopped for just a moment as he reached into his small military-grade backpack to pull out water and nutrition bars. He handed both to Molly.

"Here. The bars don't taste the best, but they're packed with nutrition. Try to nibble on one pretty constantly if you can. And water is critical. No doubt you're already dehydrated, which isn't a good way to start a trek through the jungle. That's probably why you still have so many side effects from the drugs. Drink every couple of minutes if you can."

Molly nodded and they started moving; they couldn't stop. Liam would catch up with them. But he was worried about Molly. She didn't seem very steady on her feet.

Lights were coming on at Belisario's estate, and they could hear lots of yelling. Damn it. Now they had no choice but to run, no matter what state Molly was in.

"You okay?" Derek spoke to Liam through the communication unit.

"I'm over the wall," he responded, obviously on the move. "But they definitely know something is up. It might take them a little bit of time to figure out which way we went, but not long."

Derek looked over at Molly and spoke into his mic. "We're going to be slow going. No way around it."

"Plan B?"

Plan B involved Liam, who was moving much faster than Derek and Molly to leave a more obvious trail for Belisario's men to follow in the wrong direction. He would then double back and meet them at the plane.

It wasn't a perfect plan. And it was downright dangerous for Liam. But it was their best option.

"Roger, Plan B. But Liam, be careful."

"*Moi*, not careful?" Liam chuckled, then clicked off.

"We've got to go, baby." She had taken the opportunity to sit while he'd been talking to Liam. Derek hated the way he was going to have to push her, but it was the only way. He trailed a finger down Molly's pale cheek. "Let's go. Right now."

She got up and started following him. "Is Liam okay?"

"He's all right, out of Belisario's estate. He'll meet us at the airplane." No need to tell her the whole plan. She'd just be upset that Liam was at risk. "Getting you out is the priority. He'll be okay."

Glancing over at her, he could tell that Molly didn't like it. But she took a swig of water and kept following. Derek looked down at his GPS, especially formulated for use in the dense terrain. With the shape she was in, he didn't want to add on any more distance than was needed to get directly to the plane.

He grabbed his machete out of the holder strapped to his thigh, but cutting only when absolutely necessary for them to get through. Liam would be leaving a more obvious trail for Belisario's men, but too much hacking would also make his and Molly's route apparent if the men happened on it.

They traveled without speaking. Even though the moon

was full, most of the light didn't make it onto the jungle floor because of the dense trees and bushes. But artificial light would basically be a beacon for their pursuers, so that wasn't an option. The darkness just made everything more difficult. Even so, Derek kept up a pretty grueling pace, determined to put as much distance between them and Belisario's compound as possible. They weren't running full-out, but they were moving much faster than a walk.

Derek heard a soft cry from Molly and turned, but wasn't in time to catch her as she fell all the way to the ground. This was the second time she'd tripped.

"Let's stop," he said, quickly helping her up.

"No." She shook her head. "I'll be okay. I just can't see very well."

With one eye almost swollen closed, he wasn't surprised. But she hadn't stopped, hadn't complained, had kept his grueling pace for the past two miles.

"You're amazing," he told her, meaning every word. He knew trained agents who wouldn't be coping as well as she was.

He could see her roll her one good eye. "Oh, yeah? Did you figure that out before or after I just did a face-plant in the middle of the jungle floor?"

Derek couldn't help his short bark of laughter. He pulled her into his arms and kissed the top of her head. The acerbic wit of hers was going to be his undoing.

"Drink more water." He pulled back and handed her the canteen.

"Won't we run out?"

"No, there's plenty of water sources around here. And this canteen has a triple filter system. It could make a mud puddle safe to drink. So don't drink sparingly."

She nodded and took a huge sip.

"Good." He nodded in approval. "Don't forget to eat, too. You ready to get going?"

"Yep." She smiled, but he noticed her deep breath as if she was trying to steady herself, prepare mentally.

This time he took her hand and hooked it into the back waistband of his pants. "Don't let go. No more face-plants."

"Yeah, well, you'd just better hope I don't try to get fresh with you."

There was nothing he'd like more, but knew that couldn't happen even if there weren't people hunting them. But he smiled at her. At least she wasn't stuttering. "I'll take my chances. You're doing great, honey. About eight more miles to go."

Eight miles was a long way to go for someone traumatized, injured and drugged.

Chapter Twelve

A few hours later all Molly could hear was the sound of her own breathing sawing in and out of her chest. Honestly, she was amazed Belisario's men couldn't hear it and use it to find them. She tried to make herself be more quiet, but found it impossible.

And they weren't even running. Moving fast, but not running. If they were running, Molly was pretty sure she'd have already fallen dead on the jungle floor. Her lungs were burning, the damp, hot air of the rain forest making every breath agonizing.

After an hour of shooting pain, she lost most of the feeling in her hurt leg, thank goodness. Her shoulders and face were quite a different story. Every step she took reminded her of her injuries.

But she didn't want to slow Derek down. Didn't want to stop. Didn't want to do anything that would put them in any more danger.

So she kept moving, despite the pain, despite the fact that she could never seem to drag enough air into her lungs. One step after another. Over and over.

Her hand was in Derek's pants.

She would've giggled at the thought had she any reserve energy in her body whatsoever to do so. Sadly, she didn't.

But that didn't stop her from enjoying the skin of his lower back that she could feel against her fingers.

Derek was here.

She still could hardly believe it. After her talk with Belisario yesterday, Molly had all but given up hope. No one would link her and Belisario, heck she could hardly link herself and Belisario. She would've sworn no one was coming for her.

To be honest, she thought it would be a few days before anyone even noticed she was missing. And by then, well, unthinkable things would've happened to her and she'd probably be dead. That's what she had resigned herself to.

But then she'd woken up from another lovely dream—really, a memory—about Derek. To find not Henrico or another one of Belisario's henchmen standing over her, but Derek himself.

After she figured out she wasn't still dreaming, she'd never been so excited to see anyone in her whole life. Derek was here to get her away from this horror.

Molly didn't think this could be a sanctioned mission by Omega, not here in South America at a private residence. She hoped Derek and the guys weren't going to ruin their careers by getting her out. But regardless, she had to admit she was glad they were here.

The minutes began to blend. One step after another. Over and over. Molly almost felt as if she was floating out of her body.

She was so out of it that she didn't even realize when Derek came to a stop. She plowed right into him, hit his hard back and was about to fall when he reached his arm around behind him and caught her.

He turned and put both hands on her upper arms. She could see concern in his eyes, but didn't even have the energy to pretend that everything was okay. Everything seemed to be hazy.

"Whoa, sweetheart." He helped her sit down on some cleared ground. "Looks like we need a break."

"No, I'm okay."

"Like hell you're okay, Molly. Here, drink." She was thankful he held up the canteen to her lips because she didn't think she could do it.

"I know we need to keep moving." Molly forced the words out after drinking. Derek took out another energy bar and began feeding it to her in tiny pieces. She wondered if she should feel offended that he was treating her like a baby bird. Honestly, she didn't care.

Even sitting up was hard to do now. All she wanted to do was sleep. Derek sat down, leaned against a tree and lifted her into his lap so her back was against his chest.

"Just rest and eat," he murmured against her hair.

He fed her piece after piece, bringing the canteen to her lips every once in a while. It was all Molly could do just to chew the bar and swallow.

"How much farther do we have?" she finally whispered, full volume feeling as if it was too much effort.

"A little over a mile and a half—"

They were both stunned into silence when they heard the chirp of a radio and someone speaking on it in Spanish less than a hundred feet away.

Derek spun them around so they were lying flat on their stomachs and less likely to be seen. Molly tried to understand what the man was saying into the radio, but he was speaking too quickly for her to pick out many of the words.

"Stay here, okay?" Derek whispered into her ear. "I don't think he saw us, but I'm going to circle around the back of him and take him out before he can give any details about where we are."

Molly nodded. She didn't think she could do much more anyway.

THANK GOD FOR Molly's exhaustion. If she hadn't so desperately needed a break—Derek had turned around to find her almost gray with exhaustion—they probably would've run right into Belisario's man.

Derek wasn't sure how he'd found them, if he'd tracked their trail all the way from Belisario's house or if he'd caught it somewhere more recently, but the fact that this area wasn't swarming with bad guys was a good sign. Hopefully he was alone. But Derek knew that all the man needed was proof he was on the right trail and backup would be called immediately.

He couldn't let that happen. Especially when they were this close to the plane. Derek thought about contacting Jon, but it was too risky, the guy might overhear. Plus, even if he sprinted it would take Jon too long to get here to be much help.

The guy kept talking on the radio and although Derek couldn't tell what he was saying, his tone wasn't frantic or excited so that was good. He didn't think they were around here.

Just keep talking, moron. Give me a chance to sneak up on you. Derek didn't want to use his gun, which would be heard for miles. He needed to take this guy out up close and personal. Derek considered going around the opposite side, just in case there was a problem. It would lead the guy away from Molly, but decided speed was more of the essence.

Silently Derek stalked through the jungle. His Special Forces missions in Afghanistan may not have been in the jungle, but they had still required the same patience and focus.

The man never knew what happened, and Derek had not one iota of remorse as he came up behind him, covered his mouth with his hand, and stabbed him quickly where his cranium met his spinal cord at the back of his neck.

The man was painlessly dead before Derek laid him on the ground.

And if this was another black mark on his soul, so be it. This man may have been the one who hurt Molly. Or even if he wasn't, he was in with the group who had. Derek had killed for much less reason.

He heard the unnatural cracking of a tree limb at the same time as he heard the safety being flipped off of a semiautomatic rifle behind him. Derek realized his mistake immediately. He had not checked for a partner.

But there was one. And he had either been smarter or just not as talkative, but Derek had never heard or seen him. And now his weapon was pointed at Derek.

The man spoke to him in harsh Spanish. Derek didn't understand him, but he held both hands up and got up slowly, making no sudden movements as he turned around. He still had a knife in his hand, but that wasn't going to do him any good against the weapon the man had pointed directly at him.

The man nodded at the knife with his chin. "Down," he said.

Derek let the knife fall to the ground. At least the man hadn't already shot him, which meant he didn't have instructions to kill them on sight.

"Woman," the man said. *"Dónde está la mujer?"*

Where is the woman? That much Spanish Derek could understand. "A woman? Dude, I haven't seen any women out here. I wish. Your friend snuck up on me and I got a little carried away with the self-defense, I guess."

The man was obviously trying to pick out whatever words he could understand. Derek had hoped the confusion might buy him more time, at least allow him to lead the man away from Molly, but he was reaching for his radio. Derek listened as the man reported in.

"Matalo. Encuentra a la mujer." The words came from the radio. Derek didn't know what they meant, but by the evil smile that spread across the big man's face, it wasn't good news for Derek.

The man put the radio back in its holder and lifted his weapon. Derek was about to make a dive for it—a total gamble, but better than doing nothing as he got shot—when the man crumpled to the ground.

Molly stood behind him, a large branch in her hand. She had obviously belted the guy over the head with it.

But he wasn't completely unconscious. He turned himself and his gun toward Molly in a rage. Derek didn't hesitate, but dove forward, landing on the man in a flying tackle. The gun flew from his hands and Derek pounded his fist into his face.

The larger man didn't want to go down without a fight. He got in a few punches that had Derek grunting in pain, before Derek was able to get behind him. Derek wrapped his arms around the man's neck and gave a quick twist, breaking it. The man fell dead.

He landed near Molly, who immediately backed up to get away. Derek saw horror in her eyes.

Something in his heart froze. Now she knew Derek was a killer, could kill a man with his bare hands. He supposed she had already known academically that taking lives was sometimes part of his job. But she didn't know the sorts of things he had done when he'd been in the military. The people he'd killed while his skin was touching theirs. Just like the two men he'd killed tonight.

When Molly looked over at him the horror was gone from her eyes, but he knew it would be back. This was why he had always tried to distance himself from her. To keep this blackness away from her light.

"*Matalo* means 'kill him,'" she whispered. "That's one of the few phrases I remember from my high school Spanish."

"What?"

"That's what the voice said on the radio. *Matalo*. Kill him." She was swaying on her feet.

Derek rushed over to her. "Well, he definitely would have if you hadn't clocked him. Thank you. And thank you to your high school Spanish teacher for teaching completely inappropriate phrases."

She started to smile, but then paled even more, if possible. "I'm not feeling so good."

The words were hardly out of her mouth before she turned to the side and was violently ill. Derek tried to brace her at her waist and held a hand at her forehead.

So much for all the food and water he'd tried to get into her. It was on the jungle floor now. Any fortification in her system was gone. They had almost two miles still to go and the second dead guy had called for backup.

They needed to leave now, but Molly wasn't capable of going anywhere.

"I can run," she said.

Derek actually scoffed right in her face. "You can't even stand up straight, much less run."

He took his backpack off and set it against a tree. He would just have to leave it here. "Time for a piggyback ride."

"What?" Despite how she was feeling she still managed to look at him as if he was crazy.

"Carrying you on my back will be much easier than carrying you in my arms. And much more comfortable for you than me carrying you over my shoulder fireman-style."

Evidently the thought of being upside down made her turn a little greener.

"Piggyback."

They didn't have any more time to waste. He swung her up on his back. Her small arms wrapped around his neck.

"Jon," Derek spoke into his mic.

"Damn it, man, I was worried about you. Are you guys okay?"

Derek started to run.

"Yes. We're about a mile and a half out and are probably going to be coming in hot. Someone found our trail and reported back before I could stop him."

"What's you're ETA?" Jon asked.

"I'm carrying Molly, so I'm aiming for twenty minutes. I don't have any guns on me." Talking was harder now as he picked up speed.

"We'll be ready. Liam's already here."

"Roger. Over and out."

Derek focused on running. He still had his machete to cut through brush and whacked away now that he didn't care about whether the trail could be followed.

He felt Molly try to hold her own weight as much as possible with her legs and arms grasping him tightly. But he could feel her muscles start to fail her as they got closer to the plane.

"Hang in there, baby," Derek told her.

As he reached the clearing a half mile from the plane, Derek felt her start to slip from his back, her strength obviously spent. He tossed his machete to the ground, caught her by the arm and swung her around so he was carrying all her weight in his arms.

He heard shots coming from behind them in the jungle.

"Liam." Derek hit the mic on his throat to talk.

"I'm out here and got my sights on you. Just keep running with her."

Having Molly over his shoulder would probably be faster, but Derek wasn't going to take the chance of them shooting at his back and hitting her. She was totally slack in his arms.

Derek heard more gunfire and forced more speed out of his legs. Not only did they have to make it on the plane, it had to take off. The plane wasn't bulletproof.

Five hundred yards.

Four hundred yards.

He heard gunfire coming from in front of him. That was Liam, which meant Belisario's men had broken the tree line.

Three hundred yards.

"I see you, Derek. Keep going." It was Jon in his ears. Derek could barely hear him over the sound of the jet's engines.

Two hundred yards.

"Liam. Let's. Go." Derek had no breath left for full sentences.

A bullet flew wide, over his head. Belisario's men weren't close enough for accuracy yet, but it wouldn't be much longer.

One hundred yards.

Out of the corner of his eye he saw Liam sprint up beside them, then he passed them and made his way up the stairs into the plane. Derek forced one last burst of speed and followed him up the stairs a few seconds later.

He dove for the ground inside the plane, twisting so he wouldn't land on Molly's unconscious form.

"Go!" Liam yelled and the jet began to roll even while Liam was pulling up and securing the door.

There was nothing Derek could do but hold on to Molly and pray that Jon's skills as a pilot could get them out of this. A few moments later he felt the plane leave the ground at a much steeper rate than normal, and make a sharp turn that threw them back against the side of the aircraft.

But then it evened out and they began a more normal ascent to a higher altitude.

Derek heard a loud woot and laugh from the cockpit. Jon called out, "We hope you enjoy your flight on Save Your Ass airline. Now just sit back and relax."

Chapter Thirteen

Once they were safely in the air Derek got Molly up into a seat. Her color was still pale—in the places of her face he could actually see not covered by bruises—but her breathing was pretty even. She'd be waking up soon.

Derek and Liam put headsets on so they could talk to Jon without having to yell.

"Molly okay?" Jon asked.

"She's waking up," Derek told him. "The eight miles was a lot for her in the shape she was in. Although she was a hell of a trouper."

"Looks like someone pounded on her pretty good." Liam winced.

Derek reached over to stroke a stray wisp of hair off her forehead. She moved just the slightest bit at his touch.

"Well, she's alive." Derek looked over at his friend. "And the worst didn't happen, so we'll call this a win."

Liam knew what he meant. "Thank God. I couldn't have stood the thought of that for her."

Derek's jaw tightened just thinking about it.

Molly shifted again and her eyes began to flutter open. Derek positioned himself in the seat next to Liam, across from Molly, so she could have a little space as she awoke.

"Hey, kiddo," Liam said. "Don't be scared by this ghoulish monster sitting next to me. It's just Derek. But he often scares small children."

Derek heard Jon chuckle over the headset.

He watched as Molly became more aware of what was going on. She sat up a little straighter in her seat and looked out the window, then across at them.

"We made it to the plane," she said.

"Yep."

"What is she saying?" Jon was demanding. "Give her some headphones."

Derek got up and grabbed a set, then handed them to her, smiling. "Jon wants to be able to talk to you, too."

She put them on. "Hey, Jon."

"You have no idea how happy I am to hear your voice, Molly."

"Well, you have no idea how happy I am that you guys figured out where I was and came to get me."

"Are you okay?" Jon asked.

"Nothing that won't heal. No broken bones."

"I still want to take you to the hospital when we get back to Colorado," Derek told her. "Whatever drug they pumped you full of, we need to make sure there are no residual effects."

"Yeah, that's probably a good idea." She nodded at him.

They both noticed Liam was looking kind of strangely at Molly.

"What?" she asked.

"Nothing." Liam shook his head, smiling. "That's just the first sentence I've heard you say to Derek without stuttering in years."

Molly looked away for a minute and Derek thought he might have to punch Liam for bringing it back to her attention, but then she regrouped.

"I guess my life being threatened by a real ghoulish

monster like Pablo Belisario taught me there are much bigger and badder things to be nervous about than Derek."

"Atta girl," Jon murmured over the headsets.

"Molly, what did Belisario want with you?" Derek asked her.

"I still don't know, exactly. But it definitely had to do with the explosion at the lab. He wanted confirmation that everything had been destroyed."

"Did you have evidence dealing with Belisario in the lab?"

"No." She sat up straighter. "That's just it. It wasn't about him. It was about someone he called his 'partner' and the evidence you guys brought into the lab yesterday."

This was getting even weirder. "Who is his partner?" Derek asked her.

Molly closed her eyes, obviously concentrating on her memory of the conversation. "He didn't say. He just said someone who couldn't allow me to be found on US soil."

Derek met eyes with Liam. Common criminals wouldn't care about Molly's questioning and/or murder happening on US soil. But a politician sure as hell would.

"That Secret Service vehicle," Liam murmured.

"Exactly." Derek nodded.

"Evidently this partner had a very bad day and needed to absolutely confirm that all evidence had been destroyed in the lab," Molly continued. "I was supposed to have died there. And the partner wanted the names of you guys, too, the ones who brought in the evidence."

"Whoa," Jon said from the headset. "Sounds like someone was going a little overboard in making sure he cleaned up his mess. We'd better watch our six."

"Don't worry." Molly was quick to jump in. "I didn't give them your names. They wanted names, but I told them the agents were Steve Rogers and Bruce Banner."

"Who are they?" Liam asked.

"Superheroes from *The Avengers*," Derek answered. His eyes met Molly's. Did she remember that was the movie that was playing in the background that night he'd shown up at her house? Derek hadn't been able to think of the film since without thinking of Molly.

Molly flushed and looked away, fiddling with the headset. Yes, she remembered.

"That was good thinking," Jon told her. "I'm sure you were under a lot of pressure. We appreciate you trying to look out for us."

"I'm sorry I don't have any more useful information."

Derek wanted to take her hand, but forced himself not to. He needed to keep his distance from her now more than ever. "Don't be sorry. You confirmed some important details we've been working on with Director Drackett."

Her look said she didn't believe him.

"Seriously. Even before the explosion in the lab we were considering that it might be someone high in the US Government—someone who Drackett's been reporting to—who has ties to the Chicago bombing," Derek explained.

"Oh, no."

"It's how they've kept ahead of us on all our leads, knew when we had critical evidence and knew to take you to find out more details," Liam continued. "Belisario wouldn't be able to get that information on his own. It's highly unlikely that he has any clout or inside knowledge when it comes to Omega, without his 'partner' feeding it to him."

Molly nodded. Derek could tell she was exhausted again. "Why don't you rest? We have to stop in Miami to refuel, but then we'll be going straight to Colorado."

She wanted to argue, but couldn't find the strength. Her eyes were closed within moments.

"She still has too much of that damn drug in her system,"

Derek muttered. He slid a pillow under her head where it rested against the plane.

"Not to mention the trauma of all those miles getting out of the jungle," Liam said. "She's a lot tougher than you would think, just by looking at her. I know I'll never call her mousy again."

Derek heard Jon's quiet, "Amen to that."

Derek remembered the horror that filled her eyes when that man had fallen dead at her feet. The man Derek had killed with his own two hands right in front of her.

He looked at her sleeping form. "She's strong, definitely."

But Liam was wrong, Molly wasn't tough. Nor was she hard or cold. She didn't belong in their world. She needed to be back at a lab where she could be safe. Protected from people like Belisario.

Hell, protected from people like Derek.

"Doctors will get her situated, Derek. She's made it through the worst part," Jon said.

Derek hoped so. He tucked another strand away from her sleeping face, but quickly moved his hand back when she turned toward him.

He hoped she'd made it through the worst part. But somehow he knew she probably hadn't. And that the worst part for her, was him.

Six hours later, after a brief stop in Miami for refueling, which Molly slept through, they landed in Colorado. Even though she was feeling better, Derek wanted to get her straight to a hospital. Jon and Liam would take care of the plane and report back to Steve Drackett at Omega HQ.

Everyone agreed that they all needed to watch their backs. Outside of the four of them, and Drackett, no one was trustworthy.

Molly was now hooked up to an IV and had been seen by two different doctors. Derek hadn't left her side the entire time. He'd told the doctors as much as he could without giving away any important details of the case. The cover story was that she'd been carjacked.

"Overall, I'd say you're very lucky. Neither your nose nor your jaw is broken. I imagine the swelling will go down in the next twenty-four hours and there shouldn't be any lasting effects from the blows to your face," Dr. Martin, a kind woman in her midfifties had told Molly.

She flipped through some charts. "The drug in your system is Ketamine. That's a medication mainly used when someone is having surgery, for starting and maintaining anesthesia, although it is used recreationally, also."

"Will she have any lasting effects from that?" Derek asked.

"No." Dr. Martin put the chart down and turned to Molly. "But honestly, given the amount still in your system after nearly thirty-six hours and your size and weight, you're very fortunate that you didn't go into cardiac arrest."

"Well, I've been pretty out of it since they gave it to me. Hard to stay awake," Molly told her.

"I'm sure. It's almost out of your system now, and the IV will help flush out the rest."

"How long will she need to stay here?" Derek asked.

"I'd like to keep her overnight, just for observation."

"Do I have to?" Molly sounded like a child, even to herself. But she didn't want to stay in the hospital.

Of course, Belisario's men had taken her from her home, so going back there wasn't safe. Molly didn't know where she would go after the hospital. Maybe to a hotel.

"Just for one night." The doctor had shaken hands with both Molly and Derek, then left.

Derek sat down on the chair across from her bed. "Don't

worry, I or someone I trust will be here with you the entire time."

"I don't think I said thank-you for coming to get me. Belisario…" She paused then restarted. "I would've been in real trouble if you hadn't shown up when you did."

Molly shuddered. She didn't even want to think about what would've been happening to her right now if she was still back in Colombia. "I thought it might be days before anyone even realized I was gone."

"I started looking for you as soon as I realized you weren't at your condo when I came to pick you up yesterday morning."

"Well, I wasn't counting on that."

Derek's eyes narrowed just the slightest bit and he tilted his head to the side as if the thought of not picking her up had never even occurred to him. "Why? I told you I would come get you."

Molly shrugged. "It's just, we kissed the night before. Then you left pretty abruptly."

"And because we kissed you thought I wouldn't pick you up the next morning like I said I would."

He was offended, she could tell.

Molly struggled with what to say. She wasn't trying to insult him. But he had a pattern when it came to the two of them and their interactions.

"I'm not trying to say you wouldn't keep your word, Derek." Molly tried to look him in the eye, but it was hard. She looked at the top of his forehead instead, at his thick dark hair. "It's just that after…something happens between the two of us physically, you tend to withdraw. Completely. You don't really talk to me, definitely don't touch me. You just withdraw. For months, even years."

She cleared her throat. "You're still friendly, nothing overt, mind you. But I always felt your total withdrawal from me. Maybe to protect yourself. Or maybe I just wasn't what you wanted."

She glanced down at his eyes and saw surprise. "Not that I've ever expected any commitment from you," she was quick to continue. "You never made any promises, so I'm not trying to say you did anything wrong. I'm just saying that I figured you'd send someone else to get me yesterday morning or something, because of our kiss. Because you wouldn't really want to see me. I figured I wouldn't really talk to you again until sometime next year. If the pattern held."

Derek was completely still in the chair across from her hospital bed, staring at her. Molly began to get uncomfortable. What if he didn't even know what she was talking about? He had never once brought up the things that had happened between them in the past. What if he really didn't remember?

She looked away toward the door, hoping some doctor or nurse or even one of Belisario's men would come bursting through. Oh, to go back to the good old days where she couldn't get a complete sentence out around Derek. Stuttering and stammering was much better than the hole she was digging for herself.

She glanced back at him to find him still in that frozen position. "You know what? Forget I even said anything. I must still have more of the drug in my system than they thought."

Then Molly did what any adult scientist with a PhD and two advanced master's degrees would do under the same situation: pulled the blanket up over her head.

Chapter Fourteen

Derek was pretty sure this sort of situation had never come up in his Omega tactical team training. It probably would've been in the *How to Diffuse a Bomb Using Acupuncture and Other Impossible Situations You'll Never Get Out of Unscathed* class. Derek had obviously missed that one.

The damnedest thing was, Molly was right. He did withdraw. But he thought he had been all slick about it. That she hadn't really noticed.

Evidently, not only had she noticed, but she'd recognized a *pattern*, he did it so often. But even worse, she thought it was for his own good that he tried to stay away from her. That he didn't want her.

The exact opposite from the truth.

And now she was hiding under a blanket, which Derek found adorable but also proved his point. Molly was soft, gentle, kind.

Entrenching himself in her life would be the most selfish move he could make. Derek could almost live with himself despite some of the choices he'd made in the past, lives he'd taken, darkness he'd embraced. But choosing to surround someone like Molly with his darkness?

Unforgivable.

Still, the thought that she wasn't what he wanted? That

she somehow wasn't good enough for him? It burned like acid in his gut.

He stood and reached for Molly where she hid under the covers, but then stopped. Maybe it was better this way. Derek honestly didn't know.

His phone buzzed. It was Jon.

Derek turned and walked to the other side of the room, answering it. "What's up?"

"Derek, you've got to get Molly out of there immediately."

"Why? What's wrong?"

"Evidently some new 'evidence' has come to light that makes it seem like Molly was the one who purposely caused the explosion in the lab."

"What?"

"There's a warrant out for her arrest."

Derek muttered a curse.

"What?" Molly had pulled her head out from under the covers. "What's going on?"

"Jon, I'm putting you on Speaker so Molly can hear."

He put the phone on the bedside tray and went to get Molly's clothes out of the drawer of the small dresser in the hospital room. No matter what Jon explained, they were still going to need to get Molly out of there.

"Evidently someone went over Drackett's head with the warrant. Steve is pretty furious."

"What evidence, Jon?" Molly asked. "I know I didn't do it, so I'd like to know what evidence it is someone could have against me."

"No one seems to actually know, Molls, that's the thing. All I'm sure of is that they were waiting for us when we got back here," Jon told her.

"Like someone knew we had gotten her out and was making sure they could catch her on this side?" Derek asked, bringing Molly's clothes over and setting them on the bed.

"Exactly like that, I'd say. If she'd been with us, she'd already be in custody."

Derek shook his head. "But *whose* custody, is what I want to know. Not local law enforcement's, I bet."

"Is Molly checked in to the hospital under her real name?"

"Yeah." A misstep on Derek's part, thinking that they were too far for Belisario to reach. But they weren't too far for his partner to reach.

"If this goes as high as we think it might, it won't be long before they've got men at the hospital," Jon said. "Liam is running interference as much as he can, but that will only stall for so long."

Molly had already sat completely up. Derek winced as she pulled the IV out of her arm and pressed down on the bleeding spot with a tissue. She reached for her clothes and Derek turned his back to give her privacy. He picked up the phone.

"I'm getting her out right now. We're going to ground. I will call you in exactly twenty-four hours at a pay phone." Derek gave Jon an address of a gas station not far from Omega HQ that he knew had a pay phone. He'd used it before. "We need to get burner phones. I'll be dumping this one."

"On it. Be safe."

"You, too, brother. And thanks for the warning."

Molly was reaching down to tie her shoes as Derek disconnected the call. He reached down to help her.

"I'm sorry that you don't get to rest yet," he told her as he tied first one shoe, then the other.

"I'll be okay. At least we're not running through the jungle."

She stood and Derek took his phone and jammed it down into the cushion of the chair he'd been sitting in.

"They may be trying to track us through that. Might as well make it as difficult as possible for them to find it," he explained. "Are you ready?"

She nodded. He offered her his hand and she took it. "I'm going to go out to the nurses' station to distract them so you can get out without them realizing you're gone. I'll meet you down at the end of the hall."

"Okay."

"As soon as they're looking the other way, you go."

He waited for her nod, then walked out of her room and down to the nurses. Distracting them wasn't that hard, Derek did know how to use his smile when he wanted to. And he only needed them to look away for a few seconds.

He met back up with Molly at the hallway right where she was supposed to be.

"Any problems?"

"Nope. Just had to be friendly."

"I'm sure." Her look was decidedly sour. Derek chuckled.

"Nobody else around here should know you or question why we're leaving. But your bruised face makes you pretty memorable, so I'm going to keep you tucked next to me as much as possible."

He wrapped his arm around her and pulled her body close to his. Molly kept her head down and let him guide her every time they passed any people. Most would just think she was grieving.

They were coming out the front doors when Derek saw them pull up. Two nondescript sedans, each carrying two men in suits. Derek wrapped Molly more tightly to his side and swung them in a sharp left.

"Head down," he whispered. He hunched his own shoulders so they both would just look like exhausted family members. He forced himself not to speed up the pace to draw any attention to themselves. But he did reach for the Glock in the side holster he wore. When Jon had slipped it to him before they left for the hospital, neither of them had thought it might need to be pointed at federal agents.

Derek hoped there wouldn't be a showdown with people who were just doing their jobs. They probably had no idea they were being used for nefarious purposes.

If Derek and Molly had been fifteen seconds later they would've been caught. But since the agents obviously thought they were arresting people sitting up in a hospital room, they weren't carefully watching the people who were leaving.

As soon as possible, Derek cut them into the shadows. It was a careful balance between not doing anything that would draw attention and getting them out of there as soon as possible. He felt Molly slip her arm around his waist and huddle closer.

"Did they see us?" Her voice was barely more than a whisper.

"I don't think so. They continued on their path inside the building. They probably saw us, but it didn't register who we were."

They stayed in the shadows just a few more moments. Once the agents made it to Molly's hospital room and discovered them missing, the first place they would start looking would be the exits and the parking lot.

They kept a tight hold of each other as they went into the parking lot. Derek ushered her into the car as soon as they found it.

"Stay as low as you can."

He didn't speed out of the parking lot or draw any attention to their vehicle—a black SUV. But as soon as they were clear of the main red light, Derek sped up, keeping his speed just over the limit. When he glanced in the rearview mirror he saw the blue of flashing police lights.

That was fast. Someone had made sure there was backup pretty close by in case those agents needed help. Derek smiled wryly to himself.

"I think you're safe to sit up," he told her.

"Is anybody following us?"

Derek shook his head and glanced at the police lights in the rearview mirror again, now getting farther away. "No, but it was much closer than I would've liked."

"None of this really makes sense. Why would anyone think I started the fire in the lab? And I find it very hard to believe that they had enough evidence to arrest me."

"Trust me, this has nothing to do with the lab fire and everything to do with getting you isolated. Away from the people in Omega who can protect you. Once you were alone, you'd be in trouble."

"But police officers wouldn't hurt me, would they?"

He shook his head, glancing at her for a moment before looking back at the road. "I'm sure it wouldn't be long until whatever real officers arrested you were given paperwork to 'transfer' you somewhere. And that would be it, you'd never be seen again."

"Why would Belisario send someone to kill me here? I already told him that I didn't know anything."

"Not Belisario, whoever his partner is stateside. A partner who is high enough in the US Government to get things done. As evidenced by us almost getting caught in the hospital."

"Someone in *our* government is responsible for all this? Had a part in the Chicago bombing?" Dismay colored her tone.

Derek explained about the Secret Service vehicle that had been spotted at the house in West Philadelphia.

"International terrorists attacking us is bad enough. But the thought that some high-ranking official in the government, someone people trust, having a hand in it? That just makes me sick to my stomach. Why would someone do that?" She turned and looked out the window.

Derek reached over and took her hand gently before he could help himself. "Why? Because some people are just terrible human beings who do terrible things. If you're racking your brain trying to understand it, it just means you're not one of those terrible people."

"It's still pretty inconceivable."

For her he was sure it was.

"Don't you think it's horrible?" she asked.

"Yes, absolutely. I'm just not surprised by anything anybody does anymore. Betrayal, dishonesty, greed, killing, happens everywhere."

Derek was sure she'd be just as horrified by things he'd done, choices he'd made, if she knew. He let go of her hand and put it back on the steering wheel. Right now he needed to focus on getting them to the safe house.

"We need to purchase a temporary cell phone that can't be traced. I'll use that to contact Jon tomorrow."

"Where are we going?"

"To a cabin an old friend of mine owned that he's given to me, near a lake about an hour and a half from here. Nothing about it is in my name and I haven't ever told anyone, at Omega or otherwise, about it." It was from one of the ranch hands who had worked for his uncle. Gary had been more of a father figure to Derek than his uncle had ever been.

Molly nodded and gave a tired sigh.

She needed rest. She needed nourishment. She needed

a chance for her body to heal, or at least stop running off pure adrenaline. Hell, twenty minutes ago she'd still been on an IV. The fact that she was even halfway functional was amazing.

"At the very least the cabin will be somewhere that you can rest and be safe for however long you need. To catch your breath."

"And for us to come up with a plan," she responded, resting her head back against the seat.

"Yes, come up with a plan." He smiled at her, glad for the cover of darkness, so she couldn't see that the smile wasn't anywhere near real.

Because damned if Derek, the tactical team specialist, had any earthly idea what their next move would be.

Chapter Fifteen

After stopping at a local supercenter to get food, the burner phone and some other supplies they needed, including clothes for both of them, they'd made it to Derek's cabin. He mostly came out here when he wanted to be alone, needed to get away from people, or the city, or both. The next nearest building was over five miles away. He'd never even considered bringing someone else here, especially a woman.

The cabin was sparse: two bedrooms, one bath, a living room and a kitchen. No real decorations, everything was built for function. Derek hadn't ever given the lack of coziness any thought, but it occurred to him now that Molly was here.

He didn't know what he expected from her as they'd walked through the door, both of them holding bags from the store. Not complaints about the house, Molly wasn't a complainer. Maybe just a nose turned up or a forehead creased in distaste.

But she'd only just looked around and said, "It's perfect."

They'd made a quick meal of pasta and salad. Molly was still drinking as much fluid as she could, to continue to offset the drugs and dehydration. Then, when he noticed she was falling asleep at the kitchen table, he'd shown her to the bathroom so she could take a quick shower, then had tucked her into the bed.

She had looked at him as if she had something to say, but then whatever was going on in that mind of hers had to take a backseat to what her body needed. And what her body needed was rest.

Derek watched her fall asleep as she was trying to start a sentence.

She didn't wake up for another fourteen hours.

He knew rest was the best thing for her, even more than eating or drinking, so Derek let her sleep. He did check on her, even took her pulse a couple of times to make sure it was steady, but she slept peacefully and deeply so he left her to it.

"Hi."

He looked up from yesterday's newspaper that he'd been reading through. "Feeling better?"

"Much. So much better."

She looked so much better. The swelling in her face had gone down considerably, and the bruises looked less angry. Her skin had a more healthy hue to it, not chalky as it had been.

"I'm just going to take a shower. Brush my teeth. I feel like Sleeping Beauty."

Derek nodded. "Sure." He couldn't stop looking at her.

She looked like Sleeping Beauty, or any other princess, with her rich brown hair falling loosely around her face. She normally kept it pulled back in a braid at work, almost certainly to keep it out of her way at the lab. But down like this she looked infinitely more touchable.

Derek realized he was staring at her and she was staring back.

"I think everything you need is in the shower."

Molly nodded slowly and turned away. "Not every-thing," he heard her mutter. But chose to ignore it.

Derek made more food, sandwiches this time, while Molly was in the bathroom. The cabin had seemed the perfect place to bring her, but now he realized that he hadn't thought things through completely. What it would be like to be enclosed with Molly in this small space. No reprieve.

Derek turned to the window that was in front of the sink. Yeah, she was safe from whatever might do her harm out there.

What about what might do her harm in here? Him.

He wanted to go for a walk. Take a drive. Hell, go for a swim out in the lake. Anything to create some distance between them. Physical distance. He needed to refortify. But he couldn't risk Molly's safety.

It had been okay while she'd been asleep. He'd even gotten a few hours' sleep out on the couch. But having her awake, right in front of him? What was he going to do?

Derek turned from the window to find Molly standing there, awake, right in front of him. Her hair was damp and hanging loose around her shoulders and back. She had on a T-shirt and sweatpants, both incorrectly sized and cheaply made, and blue socks.

Derek had never seen anyone so beautiful in his en-tire life.

He knew he was walking on dangerous ground here. One wrong step, one wrong word—hell, one *right* word—and he was going to start kissing her and never stop.

"I was wondering if you'd still even be here when I got out."

"I couldn't leave you."

"I'll bet you wanted to, though. Considered it. Withdraw because we had a moment."

Derek didn't want to address exactly how correct she was.

"Here, I made you a sandwich." He pushed the plate toward her. She looked for just a moment as if she might refuse it so they could continue the conversation, but then her stomach growled loudly enough for him to hear it across the room. He raised an eyebrow at her.

Molly huffed just the slightest bit at being betrayed by her own body, then sat down and promptly demolished her sandwich as well as some fruit and leftover salad. Derek ate with her.

"I finally don't feel like I got hit by a truck," she told him. "I'm sore, but I can tell that the last of the Ketamine is finally out of my system."

Derek stood and began clearing the dishes, but she stopped him. "I'll do it. You fixed lunch. But do you mind fixing some coffee? I feel like I will finally truly think the situation with Belisario is behind me if I can just have some coffee."

Molly was well-known for her love of all things coffee. "Sure," he told her. "But you're going to have to live with Folgers because I don't have any of that froufrou stuff you make at work."

"That froufrou stuff keeps the lab running, so do not knock it."

Derek made their coffee—he knew she also liked hers black—and they walked into the living room. For the first time he wished the cabin had a television or a radio or something. Anything to distract him from the fact that Molly Humphries was sitting in the oversize chair next to the couch with her legs tucked underneath her, sipping coffee. Wearing mismatched clothes under which Derek happened to know she could not be wearing anything because they'd forgotten to buy her underwear last night.

Derek swallowed hard.

"So, can I ask you something?"

Oh, yes, please dear heavens, ask him something. Ask him anything to get his thoughts away from her lack of undergarments.

"Shoot."

She paused for just the slightest moment. "Do you actually remember the night we spent together having sex three years ago?"

Derek had to give himself credit, he at least didn't spew his coffee. But it was close.

"Molly—"

"No. Do not *Molly* me." Her tone brooked no refusal. Where was the woman who had barely been able to get a sentence out around him a few days before? She'd certainly found her voice now. She set her coffee cup down. "I have spent the last three years acting like a total nincompoop around you. *Mousy Molly*. Do you think I don't know everyone calls me that?"

"Molly—"

She shook her head. "No, I deserved it. They were right. I have been mousy. Ridiculous." She took a breath, seemed to be mentally regrouping. "I thought I was going to die yesterday, Derek. In an ugly, horrible way."

Derek breathed deeply through his nose. He had thought the exact same thing.

"I was afraid." Her voice got softer.

"Anybody would be afraid under those circumstances."

"I tried to keep it together." Her shoulders straightened a little. "I *did* keep it together."

"I have no doubt about that." Just the way she'd handled

herself in the jungle, under the roughest possible physical circumstances had proved that. Although Derek had already known Molly was strong.

"Somewhere in the midst of all this, I decided I wasn't going to waste time with you anymore, Derek, wasn't going to be timid and wait. Life is too short. You either want me or you don't. I know that's a hard decision for you to make for some reason. So I'm going to help us get to the bottom of it. Do you remember us having sex three years ago or not?"

He wanted her. He wanted to yell it at her. But instead he sat back in his chair a little farther. Tried to feign a relaxed stance he very definitely didn't feel.

"Molly—"

She shot out of her chair as if it was on fire. "No. Just answer the question."

Derek couldn't sit either, but as he stood he was careful to stay far away from Molly. If he touched her now all would be lost. He walked over to look out the window. Look anywhere but at her.

"Yes. Yes, I remember." He remembered it all. Every touch. Lick. Moan.

"Was it just a one-night stand for you? You got what you wanted and that was it?"

The hesitation in her voice pulled at him. He turned back to look at her. "No. Never that."

"Then why have you been distant since then? Was it because I wasn't a better friend? You were upset that night and just wanted a friend and I forced it into something more…"

This was worse than her thinking he only wanted a one-night stand. He stuck his hands deep in his pockets. He cut her off. "Get something straight. I came to your house that night with every intention of taking you to bed.

Short of you slamming the door in my face, that was an inevitable conclusion."

That got her attention. Evidently she had never considered the possibility that he'd come there to deliberately seduce her.

He very definitely had. Yeah, he'd had a few drinks, but not nearly enough to stop him from his plans.

"Sometimes I've seen you looking at me," she said. "*Caught* you looking at me is a better phrase, and I would think I saw something in your eyes. A heat. But then all the other times you were always so distant. I never knew what to expect."

Derek had been so busy just trying to keep himself away from her, he hadn't really taken into consideration what his actions might be saying to her. She was more astute than he'd realized.

Which…he should've realized she would be.

"Molly." He took a step toward her, then stopped. "I'm sorry."

"Why?"

"For hurting your feelings in any way. For making you doubt yourself."

"Did I misread what I saw? Was it all in my imagination?"

Lie to her. That was all he needed to do. One tiny lie, let her down easy, and this crisis was averted. Moments passed. It was his tactical advantage and he knew he should take it.

But looking into her precious brown eyes, her sweet face, he couldn't do it. "No. You didn't imagine it."

She took a step closer. He took a step back.

"Why, Derek?" Her question was barely more than a whisper. "Why have you stayed away from me all this time? You've had to know I wanted to be with you."

"Molly, our worlds don't mix. I'm not the right person for you."

"Don't you think I should get to be the judge of that?" She took another step closer. She was studying him as if he was something in her lab, a piece of evidence she was trying to figure out.

He tried to take another step back, but found his back was already against the window, so there was nowhere he could go.

"Molly, you don't know the things I've done. Decisions I've had to make in the past. Some really questionable decisions."

She stared at him for a long moment. "We've all made questionable decisions."

"Not like mine."

"I know we all have a past. And I know enough about you to know that you're not still making questionable decisions, at least not lightly. You have to make the hard call sometimes, Derek. I understand that. It's part of being a leader in something as important as Omega Sector."

She took another step toward him.

"I've killed people, Molly. Not just people chasing me through the jungle like yesterday. Too many people when I was in Special Forces."

"Hard, I know. But part of your job," she said softly.

"I was always told by my commanding officers to bring the mark in alive if I could, dead if I had to. I always chose *dead*, Molly. These were bad guys, terrorists, yeah. But I set myself up as judge, jury and executioner. Every time."

"You want to lump yourself in with those terrible people, you think I don't understand, but you're not one of them, Derek." She moved closer to him.

"I once shot a man at point-blank range right in front of

his family." He was desperate to get the words out before she touched him. "In front of his children."

That stopped her movement toward him. He knew it would.

"I had orders and there were reasons he needed to die. But there were other ways I could've done it. Ways that wouldn't have traumatized children."

He turned and looked back out the window. He didn't want to see her eyes now, see disappointment or disgust or whatever he would find in them.

"Our worlds are different. Someone like you doesn't belong in mine."

He didn't expect to feel her arms slip around his waist, or her head laid against his back. "You're right. You made a bad decision. A wrong decision. And you've tortured yourself for it ever since."

She put her hands on the sides of his waist and urged him to turn around. "Answer me one question honestly, and if it's true, then I'll agree with you and promise I'll leave you alone."

He nodded.

"Would you do the same thing if you could do the whole situation over again now?"

Derek closed his eyes. No. Every day for the past ten years he'd wished he could go back. Do it differently.

"No. I'd find another way."

"Exactly," she whispered.

"But you still don't get it. No matter what, I would still kill him. His blood would still be on my hands."

"Derek, that's part of your job. What kind of person would I be if I judged you for taking lives if it means protecting the innocent?"

"But I saw your face when I killed those men in the jungle. The horror, disgust."

"Yes, but not directed at you. Directed at them. The one that almost fell on top of me had already described what he planned to do with me once Belisario was finished."

Derek was running out of arguments for why they should be apart. Both for her and for himself.

"I don't want to hurt you. I couldn't live with myself if I hurt you."

She reached up and wrapped her arms around his neck. "I'm stronger than I look. You're not going to hurt me." She pulled him down to her and pressed her lips against his. He felt her grin. "At least, if memory serves you won't."

He was done fighting this. Couldn't believe he had fought it for so long.

He took her lips with his. There was nothing soft or gentle about it. It was consumption. He kissed her in ways he'd only dreamed about doing in the darkest of nights when he'd been alone, thinking about her.

And she met him kiss for kiss. She may have stuttered and stammered around him for years, but there was nothing shy about her now. He felt her tongue dueling against his and need exploded inside him.

He slid his hands from where they framed her face down her back until they reached her hips and bottom. Squeezing, he lifted her up. Her legs hooked around his waist.

She peeled off her sweatshirt as he walked them both to the bedroom. He'd been right, no undergarments underneath. He kissed her again as he laid her down on the bed. She was the most beautiful thing he'd ever seen.

He knew he'd never be able to stay away from her again.

Chapter Sixteen

For someone who tended to be such a loner and so distant, Derek Waterman sure didn't sleep like it. Molly was still wrapped in his arms, as she'd been for the past few hours. The same way it had happened three years ago. He wanted her next to him while he was sleeping.

Not that she was complaining.

There was nothing that had happened in the past few hours that would cause any complaints from her. From him either if she had to guess.

They had wasted so much time over the past three years. Derek was stupid. She was stupid. Together the whole of their stupidity was greater than the sum of their stupid parts.

Because to think she could've been lying in his arms like this for the past three years if she had just nudged him along, but hadn't? Stupid.

"We're going to have to call Jon soon." Derek's arms tightened around her, squeezing, before letting go.

"What are we going to do, Derek? I can't hide here forever. Sooner or later I'm going to have to face these charges against me."

"I just want to keep you out of sight until we get more of a handle on who we're dealing with here. This mystery government official. I'm sure Jon is already running all of Belisario's known associates to see if he can get any names."

"I just want to do something." She got up as he did and started to get dressed. "I know Director Drackett needs someone assisting with the setup of a temporary lab after the explosion. All the cases that are stalled because of it." It was distressing to think about.

Derek crossed the room and put his arms around her. "I know. And Steve knows you didn't cause the explosion and I'm sure he wishes you were there, too. But not if it means putting your life at risk."

"I still don't like it." She knew she sounded like a grumpy child, but didn't care.

Derek walked into the bathroom to brush his teeth. "I promise I'll find you something to do while you can't be at the lab."

She looked at him standing there in just jeans with no shirt on. She'd kissed every inch of that chest in the past few hours, but definitely didn't mind just sitting here looking at it. If *he* was what she could do while she wasn't at the lab, maybe it wouldn't be so bad.

"Not me, you perverted little scientist." He stuck the toothbrush in his mouth. "Well, not just me." He wagged his eyebrows at her.

It was good to see Derek so much more at ease. Molly wasn't sure how long it would last, but she would enjoy it while she could.

"Can you get my laptop from home?"

Derek put on a shirt. Sadly. "Yeah, Jon could probably get it. Why?"

"There's stuff I can do for the lab to help get it back up and running sooner. Nobody knows those files better than I. I could access it on a neutral server and at least be able to organize some of the lost files."

"You can't do anything that can be tracked back to you."

"I understand, and I won't. This would be completely anonymous. Basically the equivalent of color-coding files, but with electronic documents. It will save me a bunch of time when I get back to work." She thought about that for a minute. "If I ever get back to work. I guess right now I don't really have a job."

"You will still have a job. Nobody at Omega would think you blew up that lab. You work too hard in it, put in way too many hours a day, to ever be the one who destroyed it. Drackett will have your back, believe me."

Molly wasn't so sure, but she hoped so. "Either way, I'd like to get started cataloging. It won't help with your case or any of the other open cases when the lab blew, but I can definitely make progress organizing past cases."

They made sandwiches again to eat, then called Jon. He was right on time and Derek put the phone on Speaker so Molly could hear, too.

"It's an absolute mess here," Jon explained. "Steering clear is the best thing you can do."

"What's going on?" Derek asked.

"Whoever the government official is behind all this is a freaking genius, that's what's going on. The whole division is crawling with Internal Affairs types." Frustration was clear in Jon's tone.

Derek muttered a curse.

"Yeah, no kidding," Jon continued. "You can't do anything around here without someone asking what it's for and which case it involves. We're in red tape up to our ears. Nobody can get into Steve's office. He's in conference with someone 24/7."

"Can you track whose office the bureaucrats are from? That would give us a good clue as to who's behind this."

"It was my very first thought. Joint task force, my

friend. Omega is a joint task force. Four different government offices involved. And we conveniently have people from all of those offices, so no hints there."

Jon sighed. "Oh yeah, Molly is considered a fugitive and a number of people are asking about you, Derek."

Derek's lips tightened into a straight line. "And damn it, we've got absolutely nothing. No clue who the government person is, no evidence left from our lead and no easy way to prove Molly's innocence."

"Thus far it seems like Drackett has been able to side-step any knowledge about us going down to Colombia. Of course, our government bad guy wants to keep his ties to Belisario as close to the chest as possible, so evidently Belisario having Molly has not been made common knowledge, nor has our rescue mission."

That sounded like good news, but honestly Molly wasn't even sure.

"It's overkill again, Derek. Just like with everything else. All these suits in here asking questions and causing delays? It's all a part of our guy's plan to keep us from getting close to him."

"Yeah, well, if he wanted us scattered and discombobulated, he's succeeded," Derek muttered. "And now we're back to ground zero."

"You should probably make an appearance at some point, Derek. Talk to the suits. Lead them away from the Molly trail. I don't think anyone has considered that the two of you are hiding out together. Molly's still the one they're after with an arrest warrant."

Derek slipped an arm around her waist. "I don't want to leave Molly alone. Not for any reason."

"I agree, someone needs to be with her. Maybe Liam or I can take turns."

"Jon, do you think it would be possible for you to get

my laptop from my condo?" Molly asked him. "If I'm going to be stuck out of the action, I'd like to at least get as much done as I can. But nothing that will link me to Omega or be traceable."

"Without a doubt someone will be watching your house in case you come back there. But I can probably find an excuse to get inside. Although if someone really did have a legit warrant out for your arrest they probably already confiscated the laptop," Jon said.

"I appreciate you trying. And bring me some clothes, if you can, okay? I look like I'm wearing a clown suit these clothes are so ill-fitting." She glanced up at Derek. "And bring some underwear, too."

"Something sexy," Derek said low into her ear. Molly shivered.

"Hey, I heard that," Jon chuckled. "Although I will pretend I didn't. Okay—computer, clothes, underwear, anything else? Too bad your lab coat burned, Molly. I'm sure you'd love to have that. I can hardly picture you without it."

Molly smiled. "Thanks, Jon. And actually my lab coat didn't burn, although it smelled like a chimney. It's sitting in my dirty clothes hamper and—"

Oh my gosh, *her lab coat.*

She wrapped her fist in Derek's shirt.

"What?" Derek said, looking into her face. "Molly, what? Are you okay? Does something hurt?"

"What's going on?" Jon asked from the phone.

"My lab coat." How could she have forgotten? "I wore it home after the explosion and took it off when I got in the shower."

"What about it, hon?"

"That evidence you gave me, when you came into the

lab two days ago, or whenever it was… *It's still in the pocket of the coat.*"

She watched Derek's blue eyes narrow. "It wasn't destroyed?"

"No. I don't think so, I didn't even check. You put the stuff in my pocket, remember? So I would know which pieces to concentrate on. I didn't have a chance to get to them that night. They should still be in my lab coat sitting in my dirty clothes hamper."

"Jon—" Derek started.

"I'll check what's going on and get over there as soon as I can."

"I know where it is," Molly said. "I can get it."

"No," both men responded at the same time.

"Jon will get into your condo and get any evidence still there," Derek told her.

"They're looking for you, Molly," Jon chimed in. "You can't go to your house."

"Well, you're going to at least need to find another lab or somewhere for me to work once he gets it."

Derek was giving her a look that said he was determined to keep her as far from any danger as possible. "We'll see."

She took a deep breath so she wouldn't punch him. "Fine." She would deal with that later once Jon had the evidence pieces and they knew what exactly they were dealing with.

"Keep us posted as soon as you can get there," Derek told Jon. They exchanged burner phone numbers, and Derek made her memorize the numbers, too. "Jon, be sure to watch your back. There are eyes everywhere."

Chapter Seventeen

Waiting for Jon to be able to get into Molly's condo was pretty agonizing. Derek had a lot more practice waiting, again thanks to his Special Forces background, than her. She was practically wearing a hole in the floor waiting for Jon to call.

He'd already distracted her—hell, distracted them both—right here on this couch, for an hour or so, then distracted her again while they took a shower. But now she was determined to focus on the evidence Jon would be getting from her condo.

She wanted to go, but there was no way he was taking her anywhere near there. Not when her place was undoubtedly under surveillance by multiple groups of people: federal agents, maybe Belisario's men, the unknown government official's men. Everyone was looking for her. And Derek wasn't going without her—leaving her alone was not an option he was even willing to consider. After the scares he'd had with her over the past couple of days, he wasn't sure he'd ever be able to let her out of his sights again.

Derek's phone buzzed and Molly immediately sat down so they could read the text. Jon was finally able to make his way out of Omega HQ and was heading toward her condo.

"Okay, so we should go, right? It will take us at least an

hour and a half to make it back into the city. Jon will have gotten into my place much sooner than that."

They had agreed, Molly using one of their *distraction* times to sway him, to go back into Colorado Springs so she could process the evidence once Jon got it. Or at least look at it and see what needed to be done. They'd use a lab at a law enforcement training facility that Liam had access to.

"If he's just now leaving Omega, he won't be taking a straight route there. He'll have to get rid of any tails he'll undoubtedly pick up."

"How do you know?"

"It's what I would do." Hatton worked for the Crisis Management Unit putting out fires, but the man still had sharpened skills when it came to subterfuge and surveillance.

They got in the car not long afterward and drove toward Colorado Springs. Jon would be contacting them to let them know what he could find. Derek prayed Molly's lab coat was still there and the evidence undamaged.

It was a huge break. The evidence in Molly's lab coat was key to everything. Those pieces were the reason why Omega's lab lay in ruins and Molly had bruises all over her face. And Derek was going to make sure he took down the bastard whose door it led to.

They rode in comfortable silence except for the tension Derek could feel humming through Molly. He wished she would sleep; her body needed rest since it was recuperating from a trauma. But he knew there was no way of that happening, not the way she was wired.

"What's taking him so long?" Molly asked once they were just a few miles outside of the city. "Shouldn't he have already checked in? Do you think something went wrong?"

"No. Don't borrow trouble." He reached over to hold her hand. "Getting rid of someone tailing you can take a long time, especially when you're trying not to be obvious about it."

"I know. This is why I work in the lab and don't do cloak-and-dagger stuff! Just give me a microscope or a petri dish and I'm fine, but I can't stand this."

"Give Jon some more time, baby. He'll be all right."

The phone rang just a few minutes later. Derek put it on Speaker. "How's it going?"

"Not good, man. I have multiple people tailing me. One was definitely government, I lost him. The other two? I don't know who they are, but I can't shake them, not by myself. They're working together."

Derek muttered a curse under his breath.

"Is Liam available?"

"No," Jon told them. "He's running as much interference as he can at Omega. Believe me, he's more help there than he would be here."

There was a moment of silence before Jon continued. "I think the best plan may be for me to lead them away and for you guys to get to her house, Derek."

Derek didn't like that plan, but he had to agree. If they wanted to get the evidence out tonight, he and Molly were going to have to do it.

"Roger that, Jon. Just keep trying to lose them. We'll take care of retrieving the evidence."

"Sorry, buddy." Jon clicked off the call.

"Looks like it's up to us." Derek changed the direction of the car so they were heading toward her house. "But I can almost guarantee you there are other people watching your house. Waiting to see if you come back."

Their best bet was to use the fact that they were together. The people watching her home would be looking for Molly by herself, but not a couple.

But he knew it wouldn't be enough to actually fool anybody watching. No matter if it was her going in alone or her going in with another person, the teams watching her house were going to pounce as soon as Molly showed up.

Derek knew there was more than one group watching. Maybe they would take each other out, trying to get to them.

As far as plans went, that was the worst ever.

The second best plan was him going in by himself. But that would leave Molly outside, unprotected. He needed to stash her somewhere safe.

"Okay, I have a question," Molly said. "Will the bad guys or whoever is watching my condo be watching my neighbor's unit, too?"

"Peripherally, maybe. But not primarily. Why?"

"Mrs. Pope, three doors down, has access to the roof through a hatch door. So does my unit. Something about fire code."

Molly's home was a condo, but the building itself was set up more like town houses. The five units were stacked side by side to each other, rather than on top of each other. Each home was tall and narrow, but it gave them all their own little piece of backyard.

"Two of us together going to your Mrs. Pope's house? That might work. We'll just keep you bundled up so you can't be identified."

He liked it better than leaving her unprotected.

"It's nine o'clock in the evening. We'd better hurry up because she goes to bed by ten, I'm sure," she told him. "She's not going to like this as it is."

If the evidence at Molly's house wasn't so important, Derek wouldn't even try something this risky. But he didn't have a choice. So they were about to go disturb old Mrs. Pope.

They drove for a few minutes before Derek found the

place where he wanted to park, three blocks from her house at the corner of a four-way stop. This would give them multiple directions to leave if one route was cut off. There were also at least five different alleys and side streets if they needed to abandon the SUV and leave on foot.

May in Colorado wasn't hot, especially at night, which was good for how he and Molly would be huddling together down the street to Mrs. Pope's unit.

"Okay, it's just like at the hospital. Stay close to me, head down, so no one can see your face. I'm going to be doing the same, because anybody watching the house may know who I am, too. Just pretend like we're lovers and want to be really close to each other."

She cocked her head to the side and raised an eyebrow. "Pretend?"

Derek chuckled. "Just stay close."

He could feel the tension in Molly as they walked down the block. Her arm was wrapped around his waist and his was down her back and resting at her hip. She was on his left side so he would have free range of motion if he needed to get to his weapon.

"Did I ever tell you I grew up on a horse ranch in Wyoming?" he said to her in a conversational tone. She had to relax or they were going to stick out to anyone looking. "I was raised by my uncle and the other ranch hands."

"Really? I didn't know that. Did you like it?"

"I don't know that I would say that I *liked* it. It was hard, demanding work every single day. Good weather or bad." He remembered many a morning in the winter when he'd had no desire to go outside whatsoever. "But the land there? The mountains? They're carved into my soul."

She nodded. "Wyoming. That's a pretty amazing place."

"And if you're good, maybe I'll let you see me with my cowboy hat on later."

She laughed and leaned closer into him. Which was exactly what he wanted. The more realistic they were in looking like lovers going somewhere, the less likely they were to draw the surveillance teams' attention for the wrong reason.

"I know what you're doing," she said as they continued walking.

"Doesn't matter. You can still see me in it if you're good." He winked at her.

They turned the corner to the street her row of condos was on.

"Okay, Mrs. Pope's house is right here." She gestured to the door three down from her own.

Molly rang the doorbell. Derek stood directly behind her, trying to block her from the line of sight of anyone else. He also tried to keep an eye out to either side of them without making it obvious he was doing so.

They were at their most vulnerable right now. The seconds dragged on. Evidently Mrs. Pope wasn't home.

"Let's go," he murmured. "She's not here."

"No, give her a minute. She's slow and she's probably irritated that it's so late."

Sure enough a few seconds later a woman old enough to be his grandmother opened the door, just slightly, chain obviously still on.

"Hi, Mrs. Pope. It's me, Molly from a couple doors down?"

"Molly, dear, what are you doing here so late?"

"Well, it's a really long, funny story…"

Derek nudged Molly gently in the back. There was no time for a long story—funny or not.

"But—" Molly switched gears "—I won't waste your time with that right now because I know you're probably getting ready for bed. But do you mind if we get to the roof from your access? I locked myself out."

"I keep telling you to make an extra set of keys, dear." Derek prayed the older woman wouldn't make this an object lesson.

"I know, Mrs. Pope, you're so right. And I will, I promise."

"Okay, come on in. I guess your friend can come, too, if he is trustworthy."

Did the woman think he was going to pounce on her?

"Thank you so much, Mrs. Pope. We're sorry to disturb you."

The woman closed the door, and after a long moment opened it again, this time without the chain. Derek could almost feel eyes boring into his back. He needed to get them inside. Now.

He put his hand at Molly's waist and ushered her inside. Mrs. Pope gave an audible sigh at the way Derek moved them all from the porch. He felt better as he closed the door behind them.

Once they were inside, Mrs. Pope got a good look at Molly's face.

"Oh my goodness, Molly. What happened to you?"

Assuming Derek was the cause of Molly's bruises, the older woman literally pulled Molly away from him and put herself in the middle. As if to make herself a barrier between them.

It was actually endearing, the way she was so protective of Molly. Until she turned a glaring eye at Derek. He had to fight the urge not to take a step backward.

"I'm okay, Mrs. Pope." Molly touched the other woman's arm. "I was in an accident. There was a fire at my work."

"Oh, yes, I saw that on the news, dear."

"Derek is one of my...colleagues at Omega. He's very trustworthy."

Mrs. Pope turned an eye back at him again. She didn't looked convinced.

"Well, as long as you're okay, hon."

Molly kissed Mrs. Pope on the cheek. "I am okay, I promise. Thank you for letting us use your roof access."

"No problem, but you get an extra key made soon."

Giving Derek one more glare, she stepped out of the way. The layout of Mrs. Pope's house was the same as Molly's, so he followed her up one flight of stairs, then to a second stairway leading from a side hall to the attic. From the attic was the door outside.

"It's a weird configuration. Obviously since the door is in the attic, it's not really meant to be used a lot. But I always liked that my unit had the access. Mrs. Pope's unit and mine are the only ones that do."

They walked around the multiple years' worth of junk Mrs. Pope had in her attic.

"Mrs. Pope seems pretty protective of you." Derek was glad she hadn't had a knife when she saw Molly's bruises.

"Yeah, she kind of gets in my business sometimes, but that's okay. I try to have a meal with her once every couple weeks or so. I know she's lonely since her husband died about eighteen months ago."

That was more than Derek knew about any of his neighbors and he had lived at his house for over five years. He had definitely never eaten with any of them. He'd never even considered it.

He stopped her as she was opening the door leading to the roof.

"I'm not sure what line of sight anyone may have with this room. Stay low and near me, away from the edge."

Molly nodded.

Derek opened the door and peeked out. He doubted anyone had done enough homework on Molly's building to know about this roof access, but he wasn't taking any chances. He took his weapon out of his holster.

Bending low at the waist, he made his way outside. Molly was right behind him. They moved quickly and directly to the identical door that was attached to her unit. It was locked so Derek had to put a hard shoulder into it a couple times, grimacing at the noise. It couldn't be helped.

The door gave way after the third good hit and they went inside. He kept his weapon in hand as they made their way downstairs. According to Jon, Molly's house was empty, but that was only based on law enforcement reports. Others would not make their presence so known.

He could feel Molly's hand on his back as he first looked around her guest bedroom, then her bedroom. Both seemed to be empty. After the noise they'd made to get inside, Derek was willing to bet no one was in the rest of the house, either.

"It's clear. Let's see if the evidence is still here."

Molly rushed to her hamper and began digging through it. After a minute she looked up at him.

"It's gone, Derek." There were tears in her eyes when she looked over her shoulder at him. "My lab coat isn't here at all. Someone must have taken it."

Disappointment was a bitter taste in Derek's mouth. They had been *so* close. "Okay, let's grab you some clothes and get out of here. We'll have to think of something else."

He watched as she grabbed a pair of jeans and some undergarments. "Can I get my favorite shampoo, too? I still feel like I can smell smoke in my hai…"

Her eyes widened as her sentence trailed off.

"What?"

"It smelled like smoke. My lab coat and other stuff I

was wearing that day. So I didn't want to put them in the hamper. So I—" She broke off and ran into the bathroom.

Derek followed and found her bending into her bathtub.

"So I threw it all in the bathtub." She stood and turned, a huge grin on her face. She held an undisturbed evidence bag in each of her hands.

Chapter Eighteen

Molly looked around the lab where Derek had brought her to do the initial examination of the evidence. *Lab.* She rolled her eyes. This could hardly be called a lab. She glanced over her shoulder at him, scowling.

"What?" he asked.

"This is not a lab. This is a…" Molly searched for the right word. "A *preschool.*"

They were at a police training facility outside of Denver. This was where future crime scene and lab technicians came to be trained.

Heaven help us all.

It was a step down from Molly's lab at Omega. She scoffed. It was *twenty* steps down from her lab at Omega. She was amazed anyone could leave this place and know how to do anything except dust for prints and tie their shoes.

Molly had the items recovered from her house on the table in front of her. Knowing they couldn't leave through her condo's front door after finding the items, she and Derek had gone back up to the roof and down through Mrs. Pope's house, explaining they couldn't get in and would need to call a locksmith. Mrs. Pope had just continued to look suspiciously at Derek and escorted them to the front door.

She felt Derek's hands encircle her waist behind her. He kissed the top of her head. "It's all we've got right now. Omega is not an option and it's not like we can get you into any police or federal labs, either. Not right now."

"I'll do my best. Let me see what they have. But I'm not making any promises."

He kissed the top of her head again. "If anyone can do it, you can."

Molly appreciated his faith in her, but she could only go so far as the electron microscope, DNA sequencer, gas chromatography and AFIS would take her. None of which seemed to be available here.

She looked at the items on the table. "You know none of this will be admissible in court. Not after the fire in the lab and me as the suspect."

"I know. But if it gets us a name, it will be worth it. Hell, if it gets us anywhere out of this dead end we've found ourselves in since the lab blew, then it's worth it." He was still standing behind her and put his hands on her upper arms, squeezing them gently. "But whatever we've got there, someone was willing to kill and die for. So it has to be something."

Molly nodded. In one bag was a set of prints. Derek had told her that the prints belonged to a man who had killed himself at the scene a few days ago. She pushed that to the side. She couldn't run them now, although she would check to see if she could access the federal fingerprint database AFIS from here. The other piece of evidence looked like some sort of communication device, although much of it had been destroyed by the house fire. But still it had the potential to tell them a lot, if she could get whatever working pieces were still left out of the melted outer shell.

She didn't want to take the evidence out of the bags

until she was ready to actually begin working on it. That meant she needed to take stock of what was available in this teaching facility.

Molly was hoping for iodine and silver nitrate to lift latent prints, but she wasn't holding her breath.

If they didn't have magnesium powder and ultraviolet light, then she might as well hang it up right now. Not to mention this place should close its doors as a teaching facility. There was no way to observe and record any latent fingerprints without those items.

She took her hair and quickly braided it so it would be out of her way. She rolled up her sleeves and donned latex gloves. It was time to get to work.

As soon as Molly began braiding her hair he knew to get out of her way. This Molly was the one he had known for four years. And she was every bit as sexy as the woman he'd been in bed with a few hours ago.

He knew not to get in her way. She was focused, albeit frustrated at not being in her own lab, and she would work the evidence until she'd gotten as much information from it as she could.

Jon and Liam would be showing up here as soon as they could. Jon had gone to his house, hoping to finally lose whoever had been tailing him. Liam would be coming straight from Omega HQ.

What Molly said about not being able to use whatever evidence she found in court was definitely true. But Derek really didn't care. He wanted to be able to move forward, not just to figure out who was behind the Chicago bombing. He also wanted to be able to know that Molly was safe. Until they knew who was behind this, she would have a target on her back. So would Derek, but he was more used to it, and more capable of taking care of himself.

Not that Molly wasn't capable. These past few days she had proven herself more than capable and much stronger than he'd given her credit for. Okay yeah, she had pulled the covers up over her head at the hospital, but when it had counted she had shown strength and fortitude.

Including when he had told her about his past.

He hadn't expected her to run screaming from the room, but he had thought it would give her pause. Pretty damn considerable pause. Not that she had been flippant about it.

Instead, as was exactly her way, she had looked at it from an angle he'd failed to consider. Derek generally did that—tried to look at situations from multiple angles to get the best possible understanding—but it was a lot harder to do when you were talking about yourself.

Derek's burner phone buzzed in his pocket. Liam was here. Derek crossed to let him in the door. Molly was so engrossed in what she was doing that she didn't even notice.

"Hey." Derek let Liam in, then quickly closed the door that led to the back parking lot of the building. "This was a good idea. Nobody will be looking for us here."

"It's the best forensic lab I could think of that might not have any law enforcement looking for Molly," Liam responded, slapping Derek on the back in greeting.

"Well, she called it a *preschool*, so I don't think she's overly impressed with the facilities."

Liam laughed. "I'm just glad we actually have some evidence to try and process."

Derek nodded. "Me, too. Were you able to update Drackett about what's going on?"

"Yes, since it's nearly midnight most of the Internal Affairs, or whatever they are, are gone. Steve looks like he's been hit by a train."

"When was the last time he went home?" Both men

knew their boss didn't have a family, but everyone needed to go home sometime.

"Honestly, I'm not sure he's been home since the lab explosion. Probably just caught a few hours of sleep on the couch in his office here and there." Liam shrugged, his respect obvious. "Where's Jon?"

"On his way. He couldn't shake his tail earlier so Molly and I got into her house to get the lab coat. Good thing, too. It wasn't where she'd remembered it being. If Jon had been looking for it, he might not have found it." Derek's phone buzzed again. "There he is now."

Derek let Jon in. "Finally shake them off?"

Jon rolled his eyes. "I must be losing my touch when I can't manage to shake five different people following me. I'm pretty sure they think I'm inside my house watching TV. I snuck out a side window and walked a couple of miles, then took a cab and walked another couple of miles. How's it going?"

"Molly's in her element. She's already been at it a couple hours. I tried to help a while ago, but she gave me such a glare that I decided I'd better leave it alone."

Both men grinned at that.

"So what is our plan?" Jon asked.

"Dependent on what Molly finds, we'll have to move from there. It's not going to be legally binding, but it is at least going to point us in the right direction."

"You're going to need to check in at Omega, Derek," Liam told him. "I have made up every story about you that I could about why you haven't been there. Hell, I even had a pretend conversation with you, with the Internal Affairs guys just a few yards away, about how you were sick and would be in tomorrow. I was supposed to bring you soup, by the way, so if you don't show up, I'm pretty sure someone will be coming to your house."

Although Liam had a great gift for storytelling, Derek was sure what he said was true. He needed to show his face at Omega tomorrow.

"And, bad news," Jon said.

"What?" That's all they needed was more bad news.

"Molly's status has been officially upgraded to dangerous fugitive. So that means even uniformed cops are going to be looking for her. I wouldn't be surprised if she showed up on the news."

Damn it. Someone was definitely trying to put the squeeze on Molly. He needed to get her out of here as soon as possible. Out of the city, back to his cabin. Jon or Liam could stay with her while he went into Omega.

Derek didn't like the thought of Molly being with anyone except him. He trusted these two men like brothers, knew they had his back, but the thought of either of them with Molly in that cozy cabin, near the bed where they'd made love all afternoon?

No, he definitely didn't like it. He'd allow it for her safety, of course, but he didn't like it one damn bit.

"Okay," he told the guys, trying not to grimace. "We'll take turns out at the cabin. We'll have to make sure we're not followed, which will be tough, but it's pretty secure. Remote. No reason anyone would be coming out there unless it's to purposely get to the cabin."

"Okay," Jon said. "It won't work for long, but the most important thing is getting Molly out of Dodge right now. Even getting pulled over for a routine traffic stop with her in the car could be disastrous. We've got to get her as far away from any type of law enforcement as possible."

Molly walked over with the evidence bag in her hand. "Hey, you guys are going to have to get me into Omega Headquarters."

Chapter Nineteen

Derek met Jon's and Liam's eyes and they all turned to her.

"No." It was in unison.

Molly blinked and looked at the other two men. "When did you guys get here?"

Jon rolled his eyes. "A while ago, Molls. I'm hurt."

"You can't go to Omega, Molly. Everyone is looking for you," Liam explained. "Things have escalated. Cops down to the last crossing guard have been told to bring you in. That you're a dangerous fugitive."

She held up the evidence bag. "There's a set of prints on here. Those I was able to get off with no problem, even with the substandard equipment." Her disdain was evident. "And I matched them to your dead guy's. I don't know who he is, but I know he touched this. I'm running him through AFIS, to see if we get a hit, but the computers are about the same speed as snails, so we should get it by the time we're all fifty."

Derek shook his head at her melodramatics. He was glad she was able to manually get the print, but Molly was right, a print didn't help them without a name.

"But this." She held up the bag and pointed at something on the communication device. "I'm pretty sure there's a drive on here that has active data. Pictures, documents or something else, I'm not sure. But I can't access it here.

There's too much damage from the fire and I don't have the equipment I need. If I try, I'll probably lose the data."

He saw how she stretched her shoulders and neck, so he moved behind her to rub her shoulders and help work out the kinks. The past couple of days had definitely taken a toll on her body.

"Fine, give it to us and we'll get the data off of it," Derek said to her.

Molly looked over her shoulder at him, and gave him a smirk. "No offense, but you can't do it."

"You can tell me how, and I'll do it. You can walk me through it. Or we can bring in one of your technicians. One that you trust."

Derek looked over at the guys to get them to back him up. But they were both staring at him and Molly with their mouths all but gaping. Derek realized it was because he was rubbing her shoulders.

"What?" he snapped.

That got their attention. "Um, Derek is right, Molly." Jon spoke first. "You'll need to let someone else do it. We can't get you into Omega. As soon as we carded you in you'd get arrested."

Molly's sigh was tired. "I'm not being conceited. I just don't think anybody from Omega can get the information off this drive except me. It's a specialization. The process is too delicate and is going to involve the use of both lasers and acid. It needs to be done in a sterile room. There will only be one chance to get the data drive separated from the casing in any sort of operational fashion."

"Even if we could get you in, Molly, there is no lab at Omega right now." Derek kept rubbing her shoulders, and pulled her back closer to him.

"Yes, there is." She glanced at him before relaxing into his chest. "The old lab, down in the basement."

Derek could remember it, vaguely. It hadn't been used in years.

"She's right." Liam nodded. "They kept it for overflow cases."

"Not that we ever have enough personnel in the lab to get to overflow cases." Molly sighed again. "But yeah, everything I need should be there."

Derek looked over at Jon and Liam. They were both nodding.

Using the old lab changed the factors quite a bit. It was in the older part of the building, less security clearance was needed there. She'd still need a swipe card, but she wouldn't have to go through a live guard to get to the lab.

"It's definitely possible," Jon said.

"Although bringing her into a law enforcement building housing a multiagency task force filled with top-trained agents may not be the wisest thing we've ever done," Liam said. "But then again, not the most stupid thing, either."

Molly turned around to face Derek and smiled. "I'm going to pack everything I need. I'm assuming that since I'm already a fugitive, taking a couple items from here won't really be a problem."

She stood up on tiptoes to kiss him, but that didn't even get her lips all the way up to his. Derek bent the rest of the way to meet her.

"Take your time," he murmured against her lips. "It'll take us a few minutes to figure out the details."

"Okay." She nipped at his bottom lip, then was gone, back to gather whatever she needed. Derek turned to watch her go for just a second.

When he turned back around the guys were staring at him again.

Liam turned to Jon and grabbed the front of his shirt.

"What just happened, Jon? Can you explain to me what just happened?"

"No, Liam. Some mysteries of the universe cannot be explained. Like how Derek finally figured out what a wonderful woman Molly is."

Derek considered punching both of them. "Yeah, you two are a regular comedy team. Like the Black Plague and Europe."

"I don't like the thought of bringing Molly to Omega," Derek said. Jon and Liam instantly got serious.

Liam shrugged. "You have to admit, it's probably the last place they'd expect her to be. I wouldn't head to Omega if I was on the run."

A thought occurred to Derek. "Is the old lab being used for cases since the explosion? If so, there will be too many people around to bring Molly in."

"No," Liam replied. "All lab work has been officially shifted to other agencies. Especially pending the charges against Molly."

"Got any ideas about how to get her in?" Derek asked. She wouldn't have to go past a live guard, but she'd still need to have a swipe card.

"Let me call Andrea Gordon," Jon said.

"The profiler?" Derek asked. He knew her, but not well. She tended to keep to herself. But then again, so did Derek.

"Yeah." Jon nodded. "I'll see if she'll let me use her swipe card to get Molly in. We've worked quite a few cases together over the past couple of years. I trust her. She already knows something suspicious is going on. I'll explain as much as I can. I think she'll be game."

"We'll have to do something to Molly to make her look a little more like Andrea. A blond wig, cover her bruises," Liam said. "She'll still need to look up at the camera when she scans the card."

"I'll see if Andrea can help us out with that, too." Jon nodded and began heading toward the door.

"You're going to need to feel that out carefully, Jon," Derek told him. "Don't tell her anything about Molly if you don't think Andrea will support this. If she decides to call it in, this will all go downhill fast."

"I will, don't worry," Jon said. "I'll let you know if she's in or not."

"Andrea was still at HQ when I left," Liam called out after him. Jon waved his arm in acknowledgment on his way out the door. "I'm going there, too, make sure there're no surprises. Give me a few minutes to get ahead of you."

"Okay. Be careful. Fill Drackett in if you can," Derek said.

"Yeah, that's a good idea. I'll text you when it's clear and Jon has Andrea's key card. Be thinking of a Plan B in case we need it."

"See you in a few," Derek replied. Liam saluted and jogged out the door.

Derek walked over to where Molly was carefully re-bagging the evidence. Concentration furrowed her brows and her long braid fell over her shoulder.

Watching her work should not make him this hot, but it most definitely did. He wished she had her white lab coat on.

"Done," she said, looking up at him. "I'm ready whenever you are. I'll be so glad to get into a real lab."

"Promise me one thing," he said to her, taking a step closer.

"I'll be careful, I promise," she told him.

Derek took another step. "I do want you to be careful, yes. But that's not what I was going to say."

"Oh, yeah? What were you going to, ohhh—" Her words stopped as he grabbed her by the hips and hoisted her up onto the lab table. It put them eye to eye. He slid his hands to cup her backside and pulled her all the way to the edge of the table, her legs falling on either side of his hips.

"I've always wanted to kiss you on a lab table," he murmured, wrapping her long braid around his hand and tugging so she looked up. Her neck was completely available to him. He trailed kisses all along her throat, delighting at her shivers.

"Actually, there's quite a lot more I'd like to do to you on a lab table and I plan to do so soon when all this is settled." He nipped lightly at her neck and she moaned.

"I never knew you had a thing for laboratory furniture," she said, wrapping her arms around him.

"Not lab furniture. I have a thing for *you* on lab furniture." He slid her even closer, still trailing his lips up and down her throat.

She laughed softly, then sighed as he nipped at her throat once more. "And you have to promise me that at least one time you'll be wearing your lab coat."

"You're pretty naughty, Agent Waterman."

"You have no idea, Dr. Humphries, but when this is all over, I plan to show you." He let go of her braid so he could frame her face with both hands and kissed her.

What was it about this tiny woman that allowed her to get to him like no one else ever had? Touched him to the point where it was difficult to think of going back to his life without her as a regular part of it?

When he finally brought his lips back from hers they were both breathing deeply. There was nothing Derek wanted to do more than lay her back on this table and show her just how much he wanted her.

But more than that, he wanted to rid them of the guillotine that was hanging over their heads. He wanted to clear her name and make sure she was safe. He wanted to make sure no one ever put another bruise on her again.

"But right now we need to get over to Omega and let you do your work."

Chapter Twenty

Molly felt like a clown with all the makeup she had on. She knew it was just to cover up any traces of the bruises, but it was so unnatural for her. Especially considering on any given day Molly didn't remember to even brush her hair—thank goodness it could be easily braided and put out of the way—much less put on eyeliner and all the other things currently being applied to her face by Andrea Gordon.

Molly knew looking like Andrea was important because of the security cameras at all Omega doors, including the older section of the building they'd be entering. She appreciated the other woman's willingness to let her use her ID card. Of course, Andrea had only done so after making a call to Steve Drackett to be certain everything about this situation was on the up-and-up.

"I look ridiculous," Molly said for at least the fifth time.

"You don't look ridiculous," Derek called out from the other room.

"He's right, you know. You don't look ridiculous, you just look a little different from what you're used to yourself normally looking like." Andrea continued putting on the makeup. "This is only so you'll look like me for whatever security guard is watching the monitors."

How was Molly supposed to ever look like Andrea? There wasn't enough makeup in the world to give Molly

Andrea's classic cheekbones and full lips, a perky nose that was just a bit crooked, like maybe it had been broken at one time. She always had immaculate makeup and hair: chic, shoulder-length blond bob.

And she always wore heels.

Molly sighed. Next to Andrea, Molly looked like what she was: a scientist who always chose sensible shoes.

But right now Molly had on a gray pencil skirt and dark blouse, both borrowed from Andrea. She'd wanted pants, but she was too short to wear any of Andrea's. So skirt it was.

Molly looked different.

"You've got a pretty pained expression there," Andrea said. "I'm nearly done. Torture is almost over."

"And it's not what you're doing. It's just that the makeup is pretty much a representation of everything I'm not."

"Good," Andrea told her. "Makeup should never be a representation of what you are."

Although the statement was true, it struck Molly as a little odd coming from the other woman, especially since she was applying the makeup with such skill. Molly realized that even though they'd both worked at Omega for years, she didn't really know Andrea. Molly didn't know if anyone really did. The woman tended to keep to herself.

"Do you have sisters?" she asked.

The question obviously caught the other woman off guard. "Um, no. Why?"

"You're just really good at doing other people's makeup. I thought maybe you practiced on sisters growing up."

"No. I had a…job when I was younger that involved makeup."

A job when she was younger? Andrea couldn't be more than twenty-three or twenty-four. It didn't seem likely that she'd had a career before the one she had at Omega as a profiler. She must be referring to something part-time in high school or college.

"Oh, okay, like at the cosmetics counter at the mall?"

Andrea smiled, but it didn't reach her eyes. "Something like that. But it was a long time ago." She continued applying the makeup in silence.

Molly hadn't meant to bring up a painful past. Time to change the subject. "Thank you for your help."

Andrea shrugged. "I'm willing to do anything I can to bring down those bastards who bombed Chicago. But to be honest, I'm doing this because Steve Drackett asked me to. I owe him, more than one."

"Well, either way, I appreciate it."

The other woman smiled and this time the smile did reach her eyes. "Okay, makeup's done. No more bruises in sight. Let's get the wig on you."

Andrea had brought a wig similar to her own blond bob. Actually the woman had a number of different wigs in the trunk she'd opened with the makeup, but Molly didn't want to ask her why after how the last questions had gone. Maybe she'd been involved with community theater.

Andrea tucked Molly's braid under a cap, then slipped the blond wig on her. She took Molly to stand in front of the full-length mirror in her room.

Molly couldn't control the little gasp that escaped her. Not only were all her bruises covered, but Andrea had done something with her eyes that made them smoky… sexy. While standing there in the other woman's clothes, with the other woman's hair, and makeup that made her face look exotic and sexy, all Molly could wonder was what would Derek think?

Even after the great night of lovemaking, Molly couldn't help but consider, if she looked like this, dressed like this, would Derek have been able to keep his distance over the past three years?

Maybe this was more of what he really wanted? It certainly would be a better fit aesthetically. Someone like the person looking at her in the mirror—poised, well-dressed, put-together—someone like Andrea should be with Derek. Not Mousy Molly.

"Whoa. Holy cow."

It was Jon. He and Derek were standing in the doorway. Jon's mouth was gaping almost embarrassingly wide.

"You look totally amazing, Molls," he said.

Molly couldn't even look over at Derek. What if he was like Jon and really liked what he saw? Molly couldn't look like this every day. Even without the wig, Molly still wouldn't look like this.

Could never look like this.

Not to mention how impractical it would be in the lab. Heels?

Plus her hair was brown.

Did Derek wish she looked like this?

Finally Molly glanced over at him. Although he was looking at her, his face was completely shuttered.

"I think it's enough to get her through a security check," Andrea said. "It wouldn't fool someone who knows us, but it will get you through the door."

Molly nodded. Yeah, she may not look exactly like Andrea, but she definitely didn't look like herself.

Derek still hadn't said anything. And Molly couldn't read anything—pleasure or displeasure—in his expression.

"All right, let's get this show on the road," Jon said. "Andrea, you've been a lifesaver. Thanks so much." He walked out of the room with the other woman.

Molly couldn't take it anymore. "So what do you think?" She gestured at herself with her hand.

He studied her a moment longer, from her sophisticated blond coif down to her heeled shoes. The shoes weren't as high as Andrea normally wore, but were still unusual for Molly.

"I think you'll pass without any problem. Anyone looking at a scanned ID picture who didn't have reason to think otherwise, would probably mistake you for Andrea."

He turned to walk out of the room, but Molly touched his arm.

"That's not what I meant, Derek." She immediately wished she had just let him go. Was she *trying* to get him to admit he wished she was gorgeous like Andrea?

She heard Derek take a breath through his nose as he turned around.

"What did you mean?" His blue eyes were cold.

"I guess I—I meant what do you think of this new look?" Damn it, now she was stuttering again.

His eyes softened at her slight stammer. He took a step closer. "You really want to know?"

"Yes." No. Why was she asking him this? She was setting him up to hurt her, and she was a fool.

He looked her over again one more time.

"I wish I could tear these clothes off your body." His voice was even more deep and gravelly than usual.

Molly looked down at her feet and closed her eyes. She knew that he would be more attracted to her like this, with all her physical flaws hidden by makeup and great clothes and high heels. Why had she forced him to tell her?

She felt his fingers under her chin. "Molly."

She didn't open her eyes, because if she did she was afraid the tears she could feel gathering might make their way out. Then she would really be mortified.

"Molly. Look at me." His tone brooked no refusal, but she still kept her eyes shut.

She felt his lips on hers. He kissed the side of her mouth, running his tongue over her lower lip, then drew back just the slightest bit. "Look at me, Molly. Right now."

This time she opened her eyes.

"Yes, I want to rip all these clothes off you. The wig and makeup, too. Because all this stuff is not you. Could never be you. And I wouldn't want it to be."

"Really?"

He kissed her again on the lips, softy. "Yes, very definitely really."

"I was afraid—"

He smiled. "I know what you were afraid of. And Andrea's look is for some men, absolutely. But I find myself drawn to long-haired brunettes wearing little-to-no makeup, generally found with their eye stuck to some microscope. Know any of those?"

"Just so happens I do." Molly could actually feel the happiness welling up inside her.

"Good. Now let's get going so we can put all this sneaking-you-into-buildings stuff behind us."

He grabbed her hand and they started out of the room, but he paused and turned to her. "I have to admit, I do like the heels. Puts you exactly at the right height for kissing." And he proceeded to demonstrate.

DEREK WANTED TO KISS every bit of the lipstick off Molly's face. Then take off all the rest of the makeup she had on, followed by that ridiculous wig and those clothes that she looked not quite comfortable in.

Then he wanted to make love to her. Her. Molly Humphries. Not some blonde, uncomfortable impersonation of someone else.

"Hey, don't smudge that lipstick," Derek heard Andrea say a few moments later.

He stepped back from Molly. "Sorry."

But smiled as Molly walked past him into the kitchen.

"I saw your aversion to how she looks. Good for you," Andrea told him.

"Nothing personal to either you or your handiwork. It's just not who she is."

Andrea nodded. "You know, her crush on you is pretty legendary at Omega." She shrugged. "But seeing you now, I realize you're the one who has fallen."

Derek wasn't sure what to say to that. He shrugged. "I just want to keep her alive and safe."

"And with you," Andrea murmured.

Derek could see why Andrea had the reputation of being the most gifted profiler at Omega. Especially for being so young. At least everything but her eyes were young. Her eyes were much older than whatever number her birth certificate said she was. The woman turned and followed the path Molly had taken to the kitchen.

They grabbed a bite to eat, some soup Andrea had available, but Derek could tell every moment they delayed was making Molly more jumpy. He squeezed her knee under the table and she smiled at him, but her smile was tight.

Finally the text came from Liam that everything was clear.

"You ready?" Derek asked Molly. She nodded. He looked over at Jon who nodded, too.

"Thanks, Andrea. I'll get this stuff back to you as soon as possible," Molly told the other woman before hugging her. Andrea was stiff for just a moment, as if she wasn't used to being hugged, before she put her arms around Molly and patted her back.

Fifteen minutes later they were pulling up at Omega. Jon drove all the way around to the farthest side of the building, far from the main entrance. Derek knew that even at this late hour there would be dozens of armed operatives inside.

This was a terrible idea.

"I'm not so sure about this, you guys." Derek had a bad feeling.

But it was Molly who was the voice of reason. "No, we've come this far. This will work. Let's just do it."

They parked and walked up to the door. Derek scanned his card first, then Jon, then finally Molly using Andrea's card. They pretended to chat while they waited for whoever was watching the security camera to buzz them in.

Now it was Molly's turn to be worried. "This isn't working. It's taking too long," she whispered under her breath, too quiet to be picked up by the audio feed.

Derek and Jon laughed as if she'd made a joke and continued talking nonsense about a football game.

But as a few more moments ticked on, Derek began to agree. He glanced at Jon. Had the security personnel figured out who Molly was? That she wasn't Andrea? Would there be agents here to arrest her at any moment?

To run now would be hugely suspicious. But he didn't want them to stay if it was leading to disaster. He reached down and grabbed Molly's hand, and felt her fingers grip his tightly. Both she and Jon were having the same thoughts as him.

Derek was about to turn and have them run, damned how it looked. He had to get Molly out of there.

Then they all heard the electronic buzz of the door being unlocked and opened. They were in.

Chapter Twenty-One

Finally, a real lab. Molly was aware of the price they'd paid to get her here. Derek and Jon, and even Andrea and Liam, were all risking their careers by getting Molly into this lab. Because they believed what she was doing was vital.

Molly didn't plan to let them down.

Even though it felt strange, she kept Andrea's blond wig on. She'd probably need it to get back out of the building.

The first thing she wanted to do was to start running the prints she'd already gotten through AFIS on the much faster computer than the one at the training lab. It should give them results within the hour.

Much more difficult was the process of accessing the data drive of this comm device. Because of the burn damage she was going to have to chemically remove the top layer of the device in order to access the drive. It was tricky, and like she'd told the guys, she'd only get one chance at it—if she didn't get it the first time, then the opportunity was lost. Molly donned gloves and set the comm device, still in the bag, out on the table.

Her operation would have to be done in the clean room, since any air particles—dust, allergens, dirt—could combine with the gasses and chemicals she'd be using and contaminate the surface area of the device, making the recovery of any data from the drive impossible.

Of course, air particles were better than heat elements. Anything remotely flammable near these chemicals and Omega would be losing its second lab in a week. But Molly wasn't really worried about that.

Unlike the training lab, this one was fully stocked and functional. Gathering the materials took Molly a little while since she wasn't as familiar with the layout, but at least everything she needed was here. She would much rather have been working in her lab. She cringed when she thought about poor David. Things might be bad for Molly, but at least she was alive.

Once she had everything ready, she walked over to where Jon and Derek sat near the door. "Okay, I'm going into the clean room. It will take me a while to get into my dust-particle suit. To be honest, I'm not sure how long the process itself will take me. It depends on how many layers of the comm device are burnt and the status and stability of the data drive itself."

Derek stood and kissed her on the nose. "Let's get this done so we can get your name cleared and you can go back to being a brunette."

"That would be my pleasure. I really hope we find something."

"Somebody has gone to way too much trouble to make sure we don't get this far," he told her. "We'll find something."

As long as Molly didn't screw up getting the data. She took a deep breath.

"I can do this."

His large hands came up and cupped Molly's face. "I have no doubts whatsoever."

She turned to the side and kissed his palm. "You won't be able to come into the clean room. I can't take a phone or anything in there, either."

"Then I'll see you when you're done."

Molly nodded and, grabbing the evidence on a special plastic tray, headed back to the clean room. First she went into the changing area on the outside. She put on her protective clothing: coveralls, boots, gloves, hood and face mask. Opening the airlock door, she set the tray with the comm device inside. She closed the outer airlock door and locked it—it was lockable on both sides—then waited for the air shower. The strong blast of air filtered through ultralow particulate air filters removing any contaminants from her person and the evidence bag.

Only after all that was done could she open the second door and exit the airlock into the clean room itself. The only sound she could hear was her own breathing. She wasn't in a clean room very often. Most evidence didn't call for its use, and when cases did call for it, she generally let someone else do the work. It was a unique experience, the quiet, the overall isolation. Molly imagined it was similar to what astronauts must feel.

The entire room was surrounded by glass except for the floor and ceiling. The table in the middle contained all the items she needed to access the data drive from the device, removing the burnt layers. The outer shell wasn't as important, since they already had the fingerprints from it. Molly used a helium-neon laser to carefully cut away the outer layer. Then using hydrofluoric and hydrochloric acid in very controlled doses she was able to eat away some of the burnt layers attached to the drive.

It was repetitive and exhausting work, eliminating the unwanted, damaged parts bit by bit, without hurting the important data drive underneath. The wig itched, but she ignored it. She ignored every discomfort and focused on the task at hand.

Until finally she had made enough of an opening in the device to carefully remove the drive.

As near as she could tell, it was relatively undamaged by either her workings or the fire. She carefully placed it into a new evidence bag. It was barely bigger than her thumbnail. Now they would get it to a computer and see if it was worth all the pain it had caused.

Molly stepped back into the airlock, closed the clean room door and began stripping off the protective gear. There wasn't as much need for care coming out as going in and she was back into the regular part of the lab in just a couple of minutes.

Jon and Derek were huddled around the computer at the desk.

Derek saw Molly. "How'd it go? You looked pretty intense in there."

Molly held up the bag holding the small data drive. "As near as I can tell it is undamaged."

"We got a hit on AFIS while you were in there. The prints came back from our dead guy."

"He was in the system?"

"Multiple times over." Jon responded, but was still staring at the screen. "And it's not good. Although weird as hell."

Molly put the drive down carefully on the table and walked over to them. "Who is it?"

"Not necessarily who as much as who he's associated with. The White Revolution Party, a white supremacy militant group out of Idaho." Both Derek's and Jon's faces were grim.

"That's not who you thought was responsible for the Chicago bombing?" she asked.

"We were considering them. We pretty much always consider them for everything. They're dangerous and brutal," Jon said.

Derek nodded. "So we were investigating them, but they were still part of a pretty long list, and not even near the top of it. But it always sucks even worse when you find out your terrorists are homegrown. Of course, it could also explain how someone in the government could more easily be in bed with them."

"Let's see if we can find out anything more useful on this thing." She carefully took the drive out and connected it to the computer equipment whose primary function was to read any usable data from a drive or any working portion of one.

Data began to flicker on the screen, plans for the Chicago bombing and then pictures.

"That's Lenny Sydney, leader of the White Revolution Party," Jon announced. "All of these guys are White Revolution."

Picture after picture of people in the terrorist group looking at plans for the bombing.

And with them was Senator Robert Edmundson. Obviously involved in the planning.

Derek's curse was angry. Guttural.

"That son of a bitch personally thanked me last week for all I was doing," Derek said. "Called us and asked what he could do to help us get some traction on whoever was responsible for Chicago."

Jon shook his head. "Offered us his personal contacts overseas if that's what was needed."

"Why would he take all these pictures?" Molly asked. "He has to know that these would be highly incriminating."

"Look at them." Derek pointed to the screen. "The way

no one is looking at the same place at the same time. The weird angle. These were taken without either party knowing."

"Somebody was trying to blackmail Edmundson, or have leverage over him," Jon stated.

Derek's phone began ringing in his hand. He immediately put it on Speaker.

"You've got perfect timing, Drackett. You are never going to believe what we found on the drive we recovered."

"Derek—"

"Senator Robert Edmundson is our player within the government, Steve."

"What?"

"I'm looking at irrefutable proof that he is tied to the White Revolution Party and that they planned the Chicago bombing together."

"Damn it."

Nobody wanted to think of someone with the caliber and charisma of Edmundson being behind an attack that took American lives.

"Exactly how we felt," Jon said.

"Well, we've got even more immediate problems," Drackett continued. "Whatever prints you ran connected to the guy from the White Revolution Party? That triggered some sort of alarm with Internal Affairs—obviously Edmundson was waiting to see if anyone would try to run that data," Steve said.

Molly looked over at Derek. The words *alarm* coupled with *Internal Affairs* did not sound good.

"What exactly are we talking about here, Steve?" Derek asked him.

"Local law enforcement are right outside the building, looking for Molly."

"To hell with that." Derek barely let Steve get the

sentence out before he responded. "No way. This is a witch hunt set up by Edmundson to track Molly down and silence her. Now we've got proof of Edmundson's guilt. It won't take a judge five minutes to give us a warrant once they see this."

"I agree. But unfortunately I'm not in charge of what is happening outside right now. I was called away from the building, probably on purpose, right as the locals were being called in. I'm on my way back now. But they're going to breech the building in the next five minutes."

"To hell with that," Derek repeated again. "What's your ETA, Steve?"

"At least fifteen minutes."

Derek looked at Molly. "I'm sorry, Steve." Derek clicked off the phone before the director had a chance to respond.

He turned to Jon. "I'm not letting them take her. I'll sneak her out or use force if necessary. But I'm not turning her over while Edmundson is still out there."

"Then I'm going with you. You can't go out there blind, alone. If she—"

Seriously, they were going to talk about her as if she wasn't even in the room? "Hey, I'm right here! I'd like to be included in this conversation."

They at least looked at her, although both seemed committed to their current course of action.

She continued, "Look, before we do anything crazy like rush out there guns blazing and just get ourselves killed like Edmundson wants, let's think this through. If you sneak me out or use any sort of force, won't that be considered aiding and abetting a known fugitive?"

"It doesn't matter," Derek said.

"Derek, it *does* matter. You both are going to lose your jobs over this, and you know it. Steve isn't going to be able to help you and even when my name is cleared there's a good chance that it won't be enough to save your careers."

"Molly, I'm not sending you out there," Derek said, tone clearly uninterested in further discussion.

Molly looked at Jon, hoping he could be persuaded to see reason.

Jon just shrugged. "I'm with him, Molls. Your life is not worth it."

Why wouldn't they see reason?

"Look, you said it yourself. A judge will give you a warrant for Edmundson's arrest immediately. Let me give myself to the police, you guys hurry up and get that warrant through, and get me out. I'll be okay. Even Edmundson can't have people everywhere all the time."

She could see just the slightest hesitation in Derek's eyes. He wanted to protect her, and she loved him for it, but he knew there were permanent ramifications for what he was about to do.

But then the hesitation was gone, determination back in its place. He was going to protect her no matter what it cost him. And damned if she didn't love him for that stubbornness, too.

"I can't lose you," he whispered.

She realized Derek couldn't be reasoned with, and Jon was just going to fall on the sword with him in some misguided bro-code pact.

Except Molly wasn't going to let them do that.

"Okay, we'll do it your way," she told them. "But I need you guys to help me get a couple of things out of the clean room. If we're leaving, it's got to go with us."

The both nodded. "Okay, then we need to come up with a plan," Derek said. "Do either of you know anything about this section of the building?"

They followed Molly to the clean room quickly. She

opened the airlock door and immediately opened the second door, without waiting for the air shower. That action completely contaminated the clean room, but it didn't matter, it was about to get much more contaminated. She stood to the side and ushered with her arm for the guys to enter.

"I vaguely remember some of this section, but it's been years since I've been over here, honestly," Jon was responding.

As soon as they were through the second door Molly went back out the first one, closed it and turned the heavy manual metal lock on the door.

Derek and Jon were now trapped inside.

She couldn't hear inside the room, but she saw Derek's face as he stopped talking to Jon and looked over at the closed door. His eyes narrowed as he walked quickly through the airlock to the outer door, and realized it was locked.

His fist came up and slammed against the thick glass of the door. Molly startled even though she could barely hear the sound. Fury was written on every aspect of his features. He spoke to her through the glass—angry words—but she couldn't tell what he was saying. Based on his face, she was glad.

He couldn't get out; the clean room seconded as a bomb disposal area and could withstand a relatively large explosion, so hitting or even shooting at the glass wasn't going to help Derek.

She saw him get himself under control and look her in the eyes. He mouthed the word *open*.

She shook her head no.

He flattened both his hands against the glass.

Molly, please.

She walked closer to him, wanting to let him out, but knowing she couldn't.

"I can't lose you," she repeated his words back to him. But it was the truth.

She didn't know if he could understand her, but couldn't stay to find out. She turned back around and walked out the door of the lab and the building, taking off her blond wig as she went. Colorado Springs Sheriff's officers were everywhere. Lights were blazing in the husky dawn light.

She raised her hands far in the air. "My name is Molly Humphries and I am surrendering. The two agents I took captive are inside, unharmed."

She heard the sound of guns being cocked and knew they were pointed at her. As two officers rushed up to her and forced her onto the ground and put her hands behind her back to cuff them she hoped she wasn't making the worst mistake of her life.

Chapter Twenty-Two

As soon as Molly walked out the door, Derek did what he did best: worked the problem. He immediately called Steve Drackett.

"Molly just surrendered to local PD and whoever else is out there," Derek told his boss with no greeting whatsoever.

"Good. That was the best thing to do. I was afraid you were going to do something completely asinine like try to get her out using force. That would not have been a good idea."

"Yeah, well, that was my plan. But she locked us in the clean room and went out on her own."

"She probably saved you a couple of years in prison, not to mention your career."

"Damn it, Steve, I would've gladly spent a couple years in prison, if it would save her life!"

"Molly, as usual, is thinking more clearly than anybody else in the room, it sounds like. This is not a dichotomy, Derek. We know the danger she's in. We can protect her."

Derek rubbed a hand over his face. God, he hoped what Steve said was true. "Get some agents on her, Steve. Right now."

"I've already got three on her. Nothing is going to happen. And the chief of police in Colorado Springs is a personal friend. I will make sure he's apprised of the situation and knows that Molly is not to be handed over to anyone, short of a presidential order."

Derek didn't like Molly being out of his care, but he knew Drackett was right—she'd probably just saved him, or at least his career. He'd thank her as soon as he throttled her.

As soon as she was back safely in his arms.

"We need to start the warrant on Edmundson."

"I already have someone in the office working on the initial paperwork. I'll be there in five minutes. We'll get you out and get Molly."

Derek gripped his phone tighter. "Hurry."

"You just hang tight," Steve told him. "Oh yeah, I guess Molly didn't leave you much choice." He chuckled.

Derek clicked off the phone. Everybody was a comedian.

"Is he on his way?" Jon asked, leaning against the worktable in the middle of the room.

"Yeah. Five minutes."

"I can't believe she locked us in here," Jon continued. "I didn't even see it coming."

"Drackett thinks she kept the two of us out of jail, but she and I are still going to have words about this."

And by *words* he meant he was going to keep her in bed for a week until she promised never to do anything to potentially threaten her life ever again. But Jon probably didn't need to be privy to that info.

True to his word, Drackett, surrounded by a dozen of Colorado Springs' finest, entered the lab just a few minutes later. The police searched the room while Drackett let Derek and Jon out of Molly's prison.

"She's on her way to the station," Steve told Derek

immediately. "Our agents are providing reports every fifteen minutes."

"I'm going there," Derek said.

Drackett stepped in front of him. "No, you have to stay here, get things going with the Edmundson arrest. It's all I can do to convince them that you're not to be arrested with her, Derek. They're not going to let you anywhere near her at the station."

"He's right, man." Jon popped him on the shoulder with the back of his hand. "You can do more good for her here. Let's go."

Derek was still torn.

"Updates every fifteen minutes," Steve reminded him.

Derek nodded, hoping he wasn't making a mistake he'd regret for the rest of his life.

But as the day went on, Drackett's people reported in at the promised intervals, assuring Derek of Molly's well-being and even sending pictures every once in a while. Although she looked uncomfortable, bored and tired, she at least was safe.

Derek could admit to his petty pleasure that she looked miserable in the pictures. Good.

Drackett called in a favor and woke a federal judge even though it was early in the morning. The information on Edmundson and the White Revolution Party was sent to him electronically and within the hour the warrants had been signed for the arrest of the leaders of the white supremacy group as well as Senator Edmundson.

Derek just wished the son of a bitch was here in Colorado, so he could arrest him himself. But he was in Washington, so the local feds were being called in to make the arrest. The arrest would be quiet, of course.

Because this was a terrorist attack, under the Patriot Act he could still be arrested even though these photos probably couldn't be used in court. Hopefully the photos would be enough to get a confession. Either way, every law enforcement agent in the country would be searching for evidence that would further tie Edmundson to the bombing.

That bastard could expect to spend the rest of his life behind bars. If he was lucky.

Liam and Andrea had come in to help in whatever way they could. Jon and Steve were currently poring over the pictures and data found on the drive. Derek was putting in calls to figure out exactly what evidence was held against Molly that had her being detained across town. Nobody seemed to know. Nor could anyone produce a warrant with an actual signature for her arrest.

That would be because there was no evidence linking her to the lab explosion and probably no real warrant.

A video call came through in the conference room where they were all working. Congressman Donald Hougland. Although Steve answered the call, Derek completely turned his back on the man. He didn't have time for yet another speech about how he wasn't doing his job right and as part of *the best of the best*, he should be doing better.

Steve tried to waylay the congressman completely upon answering. "Congressman Hougland, right now is not a good time. We've had a significant breakthrough in the Chicago—"

The congressman held up his hand. "I just heard about Robert. I've known him for years, and have seen him make some questionable judgments for what he thought were good reasons, but this is beyond unforgivable."

Derek turned back around to look at the man. At least he was being reasonable this time.

"Congressman—" Steve started again.

"No, just let me finish. I know some harsh things have been said about your competency over the past few days.

It ends up someone was deliberately hindering your progress, which is sabotage, not ineptitude. So I apologize for my remarks. I was wrong."

"Thank you, Congressman Hougland. Everyone here appreciates that, I'm sure."

The older man laughed. "But they've got work to do, I know, I know. And while they don't want to be rude—or maybe a few do—" he looked directly at Derek "—they don't really want to talk to me. Understandable. Keep up the good work, everyone." Hougland disconnected.

Derek appreciated Congressman Hougland's statement more than the man probably knew. Someone willing to admit when they were wrong, publicly, was the type of person needed in government office.

But right now, he just wanted to make sure Molly got out of that police station. The work was tedious, proving up the chain at multiple agencies that there was no actual evidence on Molly, nor was anyone in possession of a signed, original warrant for her arrest.

Without the warrant, the police couldn't hold her. "Steve, I've traced the stuff on Molly and nobody has a signed warrant. It looks like all the agencies were just following each other with the APB put out on her. Nobody actually questioned it."

"Good," Drackett said. "I'll call Brandon Han and send him over. He'll have her out in no time."

Brandon was a fellow agent and gifted profiler, who also held a degree and license to practice law. The man could run circles mentally around most people. Derek was sure he wouldn't have any trouble getting Molly released.

For the first time since she'd walked away from him in the lab, Derek could feel the pressure in his chest easing. She was going to be okay. Whatever plans Edmundson had for taking her had been thwarted.

But the plans Derek had for her? Those were definitely not thwarted and she was in so much trouble. Spending at least the next two days with her tied to his bed until she saw the error of putting herself in danger ought to be a good start. Derek grinned and had to shift a little in his chair from the way his whole body tightened.

But that was tonight. Right now there was so much paperwork to be done—the necessary, but boring part of any member of Omega Sector's job—it would take the rest of the day to put even a slight dent in it.

After all, it wasn't every day that you were behind the arrest of a US senator. The evidence they had on the leader of the White Revolution Party was more circumstantial, but Derek was willing to bet Edmundson would roll over on everyone at the White Revolution Party if it kept him off death row.

But something about all this was bugging him. Obviously the White Revolution Party and Edmundson had partnered together on the bombing. These pictures were almost irrefutable evidence of that. Not only of pictures of them together, but of them together looking at plans.

The problem was why these pictures and info even existed in the first place. Their existence was not in Edmundson's nor the White Revolution Party's best interest, so they definitely hadn't taken them, or if they had it had been for blackmail purpose.

But Edmundson had known the data drive with the photos existed because he'd blown up the lab rather than have its contents come to light. Understandably so, now that its contents had been made public.

But how had the drive come into existence in the first place? It didn't matter for the purpose of Edmundson's arrest, but it would need to be answered.

Three hours later Drackett got the news Derek had been waiting for and immediately relayed it to Derek.

Molly was out. Safe. Brandon Han was giving her a ride home since she was exhausted and—Steve had written it down so he could get it right—"knew Derek was going to blow all of this out of proportion and she just didn't want to deal with him yet."

Everyone snickered at that.

Maybe three days tied to his bed…

Derek rolled his eyes. "Thanks for the exactness, boss."

Steve smiled. "Just part of my job."

It was late afternoon by the time they were all ready to call it quits. Things weren't wrapped up, but at least the events set in motion by them today could carry on without their direct supervision. It was time to go home. No one had gotten a full night's sleep since the lab explosion nearly five days ago. At least tomorrow was Sunday.

"Molly and I probably won't be here on Monday." Derek told Steve on their way out. "She still needs some recoup time from what happened to her at Belisario's compound." Not to mention that Derek had plans for her that very definitely did not involve Omega.

Steve nodded. "I understand."

"I sent those pictures and all the info from the data drive to you via email," Jon told him. "Just in case you guys are looking for something to do."

"Yeah. We won't be." Derek slapped Jon on the back. "See you guys Tuesday."

Derek drove to his house, willing to give Molly a little more time before he went over there and "blew everything out of proportion." Oh, she had no idea. He'd take a shower, grab a change of clothes and head over to her place. He didn't plan to come back here until Tuesday.

Derek clicked on his computer while putting on his

clothes after his shower. He would take the laptop with him although he didn't plan to spend much time, if any at all, looking at it. He had better things to do.

He uploaded the email Jon had sent with the pictures, so they'd be readily available. He'd need to study them all in close detail later. He was just shutting the computer down when one picture caught his attention.

The man in the corner with Edmundson. He was obviously part of Edmundson's inner circle. But Derek recognized him.

He'd killed him in the jungle near Belisario's house.

This man worked for Edmundson, but obviously worked for Belisario, too. What did that mean? Some sort of double cross? Was Belisario the one who had taken the pictures? To use for blackmail?

Or maybe they'd underestimated Belisario's involvement all along. They'd taken him at his word when he'd said he was questioning Molly for his "partner."

But maybe Belisario wasn't just doing Edmundson's dirty work. Maybe Belisario had a lot to lose also if Molly had discovered and reported the evidence.

Derek grabbed his phone. Jon and Steve had already left the office, but someone would still be there. Derek would email Steve about his theory, but he wanted to make sure someone was already looking into Belisario right away.

Liam answered the phone in the conference room they'd all been working in. Perfect. Liam knew the most about Belisario from his time in Vice. Derek explained what he'd seen in the picture, confirming his theory about Belisario being a key player in the bombing.

"It would be a perfect cover-up," Liam agreed. "A white supremacy group working with Latinos? No one would've been looking for that pattern."

"Definitely."

"Hang on, a report about Belisario came across my desk a couple hours ago, but I haven't had a chance to look at it."

A moment later Liam let out a curse.

"What?"

"Report says Belisario's not at his house, Derek. That he left this morning around seven o'clock in a plane."

Damn it. That was right after Molly got arrested. "Do we know where he was going?"

Liam's curse was ugly. "Colorado. The DEA's inside informant said Belisario mentioned he was coming to Colorado." Derek picked up his home phone while still on the line with Liam on his cell and called Brandon Han's number since Molly didn't have a phone right now. Han's phone immediately went to voice mail.

"Liam, has Brandon checked back in?" He finished tying his shoes while he waited for Liam to check if Brandon's ID had been swiped anywhere in Omega.

"He's not here, Derek. Nowhere in the Omega facility."

"And I just called his phone. He's not answering."

"Let me ping his phone, check his location."

Derek was already running toward his front door.

"He's at Molly's condo."

"I'm on my way there now. Get Jon and Steve and meet me there. But keep this quiet. No locals," Derek told him as he jumped into his car and pulled out of his driveway, tires squealing. He disconnected and threw his phone down in the passenger seat.

Belisario was here in Colorado because he wanted to tie up loose ends.

That loose end was Molly.

Chapter Twenty-Three

All Molly wanted to do was go home, take a shower, sleep and see Derek. Not necessarily in that order.

After the fourth hour of sitting in that interrogation room, with nobody having come in to see her, Molly had been pretty sure she'd made a mistake by turning herself in. How long could they keep her there? Indefinitely? Molly wasn't sure exactly what the rules were when it came to a case that was tied to a terrorist attack. She was pretty sure they were different from a regular case. Maybe she'd die of starvation or old age or boredom right in the room.

She had thought she would be questioned, but apart from the first officers who had brought her in, no one had asked her anything. Which was a little disappointing since she had been looking forward to rebutting whatever evidence had been found against her. Molly worked with evidence all day every day. If anyone could prove evidence was false, it was she.

But they never brought it.

After what seemed like a million hours, there had been a brief knock on the door before Brandon Han stuck his head in.

"Hi, Molly. Steve Drackett asked me to put on my lawyer suit and come get you out. Are you doing okay?"

Molly could've kissed his beautiful Asian face, but he

probably wouldn't have appreciated it. He was a pretty straight-laced guy, not to mention one of the most brilliant around Omega.

"Yes, I'm fine. Just tired and bored."

"I understand." His nod was sympathetic. "It shouldn't be too much longer. I'm filing the paperwork for your release and since no one can find an actual arrest warrant, I'm betting they'll be pretty quick to let you go."

"Great. I'm ready."

"Well, nothing is ever quick when it comes to paperwork at a police station, but I'll be back as soon as I can."

That ended up being another two hours.

But now Molly was out. And Brandon told her that Senator Edmundson had been arrested. So it sounded as if everything had worked out the way it should.

She wondered if Derek was still mad at her. Hopefully she could make him understand why she'd had to do it.

Brandon gave her a ride home, stopping by a fast-food place on the way.

"Do you want to go by Omega or just straight home?" he asked her.

"Home, I guess. Derek is going to blow all of this out of proportion. I don't think I want to deal with him yet."

Brandon raised an eyebrow. "Yeah, you know Waterman. Legendary for blowing everything out of proportion."

Nothing could be further from the truth. But Brandon called it in to Steve Drackett as they drove to Molly's condo.

Brandon parked. "I'm just going to come in and check out your place real quick, if that's okay."

Molly was relieved. After the week she'd had, a friendly presence inside her home was welcome.

Molly stood against the inside of the front door while Brandon inspected the rest of the house.

"Looks clear," he told her, smiling, when he returned. "Do you want me to stay with you? Until Derek, or somebody else, if you really don't want to deal with him, can get here?"

Molly didn't want to be a coward. She was going to have to be alone in her home sometime. It might as well be now. "No, with Edmundson already arrested, I think I'm safe. But thanks for the offer."

"No problem." Brandon reached to open the door. "But don't stay here alone if you get scared. Call Derek, or me, or anyone. Post-traumatic stress is a real—"

Brandon's words were cut off as the door burst open. The butt of a gun cracked him in the head before he could do anything and Brandon fell to the floor unconscious.

Pablo Belisario strode into the room, followed by two of his goons. One shut the door while the other grabbed Molly.

Molly was so flooded by terror, remembering what had happened the last time she'd been in Belisario's presence, she couldn't even fight. Not that she could do much damage to the much bigger man holding her.

They backed her away from the door toward her kitchen. Brandon was lying on the floor unmoving.

"What do you want me to do with him, boss?" the man asked Belisario. "Kill him?"

"Not just yet, but tie him up," Belisario told him, then turned to Molly. "It might end up that the agent can be of some use to us alive. We can always kill him later."

Belisario walked over to Molly and grabbed her chin. She tried to pull away, but his fingers sank painfully into her jaw. The man holding her arm gripped her tighter, also.

"Of course, keeping someone alive can occasionally come back to haunt you," Belisario continued, giving her face a brutal shake. "For example, I was supposed to kill you, but I didn't. And here you are causing all sorts of trouble."

It was clear that Belisario did not plan to make the mistake of keeping her alive twice. Through the haze of fear, Molly tried to figure out why he hadn't already done it. Why he'd come here himself. But as long as she was still alive, she was going to at least try to make the man see reason.

"Mr. Belisario." Molly's words came out funny because of how he held her face. "We found evidence, but nothing had anything to do with you. It was all concerning Senator Edmundson. Evidently, he was working with the White Revolution Party in the Chicago bombing a couple weeks ago."

Belisario released her chin and tilted his head at the man holding her arm. He threw Molly down into one of the chairs at her kitchen table.

"White Revolution Party, the white supremacy group? What a shame the senator got caught up with people like them." He tsked and shook his head. "But sometimes you have to do business with people you find distasteful."

There was obviously something Molly didn't understand here, a vital piece of information she was missing. And it all came down to what could be important enough that Pablo Belisario would be here, in Colorado, himself. That would happen only under the most dire of circumstances, she was sure.

And then the obvious truth hit her. "You're part of the Chicago bombing, too."

"So clever." He touched her on the cheek and Molly cringed away. "I guess I should expect that from a scientist."

"There's something on the data drive that incriminates you also."

"The Chicago bombing was *my* plan. Edmundson already had ties to the White Revolution Party long before that happened. But he was key to me being able to do business with them. They are white supremacists after all, and I am Latino. Ignorance of that magnitude is so difficult to swallow."

"But why would you want to perpetrate a terrorist attack on Chicago? On anywhere in the United States? What would you stand to gain?"

"Interestingly, the White Revolution Party, Edmundson and I were all united on that one point—we all wanted the US Government focused on terrorists and international threats. Something like this happens and everyone in the government gets thrown into a tizzy. Money is flung everywhere."

Belisario's smile made Molly's skin crawl. "Edmundson wanted the government to propel money toward whatever he was trying to get funded. I don't know exactly what it was, and I don't care. He called himself a 'patriot who was willing to slaughter a few to protect the many.'"

He leaned down close to her. "The White Revolution Party and I realized that every time the national focus is on solving some big attack, or finding some elusive Middle Eastern terrorist group, less focus is on us and our activities. I've been able to move billions in product since the bombing, easier than ever before.

"The three of us working together made a perfect triangle. The White Revolution Party planned and created the bombs, since they had the means and knowledge, but they couldn't actually plant them because of how they are watched by federal agents all the time. I had no knowledge of how to make bombs or where to put them, but was not being watched for this sort of activity, so my men could plant the explosives."

His face, only inches from hers, was almost giddy with his own self-importance.

"And Edmundson handled misdirecting the investigation away from you or the WRP," Molly finished for him.

"Exactly." He stood straight again.

"It was a good plan." Molly had to admit it. She also had to admit to herself that there was no way she was leaving this house alive. Not with all the knowledge she now had about Belisario.

Molly had no idea how to get herself out of this. As long as Belisario kept monologuing, she was relatively safe, but that couldn't go on forever.

"But something went wrong, didn't it?"

Belisario's lips tightened into a thin line. "No honor among thieves. That's the saying, is it not? I knew I could not trust either party I found myself partnered with, but especially Edmundson. It would be just like him to try to make himself the hero by proving the White Revolution Party and I worked together on the bombing. Thus the drive with all the pictures of the WRP leadership and Edmundson together."

Out of the corner of her eye Molly saw Brandon shift slightly on the floor, then still himself. Maybe he was awake.

"Ends up my instincts were correct. Edmundson was already giving signs of double-crossing me, threatening to lead law enforcement my way. So I decided I best show Edmundson the damning evidence I had on him, although I didn't necessarily plan to use it."

"The pictures," Molly whispered. She tried to shift farther away on her chair, but a hand instantly clamped down on her shoulder.

"Yes. But then the WRP found out we were meeting and got nervous and sent their own representatives. And that's when your Omega agents caught the trail. The drive wasn't destroyed in the fire and the WRP man was killed.

"Edmundson hired someone to blow up the lab when we learned the drive wasn't destroyed. And asked me to question you to make sure all the data had been eliminated."

Belisario shook his head as if in disbelief. "Despite all our attempts otherwise, that drive is still in the hands of law enforcement. Unfortunately, with Edmundson out of the picture I no longer have a foothold in law enforcement. But I don't need it, because I have you."

"M-me?" Molly stuttered. Although it sounded like a good thing, it was bad. Really bad.

"There are, unfortunately, a couple of photos on the drive that are incriminating for me. One of my men that I had placed within the WRP was in one of the photos. You, and the men who rescued you from my estate, are the only ones who can make the link between him and me."

He smiled almost sweetly at her.

"I need you to call your friends and tell them to come here. Right now."

"But…" Molly did not want to call Derek and invite him to his death. "There were, like, twenty people who rescued me."

The blow from Belisario knocked her off her chair. The world spun as the guy behind her picked her up and plopped her back in the chair.

"That was for the lies, the made-up names you gave me before," Belisario said. He turned and pointed at Brandon Han. "Bring him over here."

They dragged the agent over to the table. Blood was oozing from the wound on his head just behind his ear.

Belisario pulled out a gun elongated by its silencer and pointed it at Brandon's head.

"We know there were two men who broke in to the

estate that night. You will contact them right now, or I will kill this man."

Brandon's brown eyes looked at her, but he didn't say a word.

"One."

Could she trade Brandon's life for Derek's?

"Two."

"Okay, stop!" Molly yelled. "I will call him. But I don't have a phone."

"See, he did come to some use, didn't he?" As if they were having a genteel conversation about dinner plans, Belisario handed her his phone. "By all means, use mine."

She dialed Derek's burner phone number—thank God he had forced her to memorize the new number—and listened as it rang. She thought he wasn't going to pick it up, which would at least take this impossible situation out of her hands.

"Waterman."

"Derek, it's Molly."

"Molly, are you okay? Where—"

Belisario snatched the phone out of Molly's hand. "Derek Waterman is it?"

"Belisario." Molly could hear Derek's voice even though she didn't have a phone up to her ear.

"Oh, good, you know who I am. I will make this very easy for you, Mr. Waterman. I have the lovely Ms. Humphries right here with me at her house. Hold just one moment, please." He put the phone on her table and extended his hand out to Molly. She reluctantly placed her hand in his. When he brought it up to his lips, she barely restrained her cringe.

But then he turned her hand around in his and calmly yanked sideways while twisting on her pinky.

Molly felt the bone break.

White dots flashed in front of her eyes and she let out a scream at the unexpected searing pain. Only the thug behind her with his grasp on her shirt kept her upright in the chair at all.

She saw Brandon stand up and lunge across the table, even with his hands tied, before he was roughly thrown back down by the other man and slugged in the face for his efforts.

Molly tried to get her breathing under control, but could only seem to sob as she cradled her wounded hand to her chest. Belisario brought the phone back up to his ear.

"Now, now," he laughed. "Is that the language becoming of a federal agent? Hold just a moment and let me put you on Speaker so you and Ms. Humphries can hear each other more easily."

Molly knew Belisario wanted her in hysterics to motivate Derek to do what he asked. But even knowing it, she couldn't seem to stop sobbing.

"Molly? Molly, baby, hang in there," Derek said. "I'm coming, okay?"

"That was her pinky, Mr. Waterman," Belisario told him. "I will break another of her bones every ten minutes until you and the other man who was with you at my estate arrive. Alone."

"I've got to find Liam, and I'm across town, you bastard. There's no way I can get there in less than thirty minutes."

"Unfortunately, then, it seems like Ms. Humphries will have three more broken bones by that time."

Belisario smiled at Molly and disconnected the call.

Chapter Twenty-Four

Derek was going to kill that son of a bitch.

He hit the side button on his watch so he had an exact countdown for the time. Because he was sure Belisario would be true to his word about every ten minutes.

Molly's scream as that bastard broke her finger would haunt Derek for a long time. He was still sweating even though the weather was mild. Adrenaline coursed through him.

He was ready to fight.

Liam was on his way, as were Jon and Steve. He estimated Liam's arrival would be in another ten minutes. Jon and Steve's sometime after that, depending on where they were when Liam was able to contact them.

Derek had told Belisario it would take him thirty minutes to get there. He'd lied.

He was already on the roof of Molly's house. And he'd be damned if he was going to let another of Molly's bones be broken.

Eight minutes.

Mrs. Pope had been very surprised to see him when he'd knocked on her door a few minutes ago. He'd shown her his badge. "Molly's in trouble, Mrs. Pope. I need to use the roof access to get her away from the bad people who have her."

He'd expected hysterics, expected her threatening to call the police, expected to have to traumatize the old woman by locking her in a closet.

Instead she'd let him in saying, "Is it like that remake of the *Hawaii Five-O* show? I love that program. I watch it every week."

"Yes, ma'am. Something just like that." He smiled and quickly made his way up the stairs.

"Book 'em, Danno," she'd called after him, giggling like a schoolgirl.

Booking had been the plan before Belisario had decided to start torturing Molly. Now all bets were off.

Seven minutes.

Derek dialed Liam's number. "Bastard called me. Said he would break one of Molly's bones for every ten minutes it takes you and me to get to him."

"Do you believe him?"

"I heard him break one already."

Liam let out a blue streak, which matched Derek's feelings exactly. "I'm five minutes out."

Five minutes was cutting it close to the next deadline.

"There's roof access to her condo. I'm already on it. They won't be expecting me coming from this way or this early."

"Is Han in play?"

Brandon Han was not only the smartest guy they all knew, he was wicked good in hand-to-hand fighting. Black belt in all sorts of martial arts. But if he was dead or injured, he wouldn't be any help to them.

"Unknown. We can't count on him."

Six minutes.

"I'll get in position," Derek told him. "You ring the doorbell. They won't be expecting it to be us this soon. You take out whoever is at the door, I'll try to take out the rest."

"We don't know how many are in there, Derek. We may be way outnumbered."

"I know. But I also know that Belisario has no intentions of letting any of us leave alive anyway. We may as well go down fighting if we have to go down."

Derek grimaced. Molly would be right in the middle of the firefight.

"Jon and Steve are about ten minutes behind me. I'll tell them to just come in hot. Might as well add more partygoers to this throwdown. See you soon, brother. Be careful."

Derek heard the car speed up as Liam disconnected.

Five minutes.

The roof door was still broken from where they'd gotten in yesterday, so Derek inched it open as quietly as possible. The element of surprise was his only tactical advantage.

Weapon drawn, he eased down the steps, opened the door that led into Molly's hallway. No one seemed to be upstairs, but Derek checked again, just in case. Although taking someone out without notifying everyone downstairs of his presence would be just about impossible.

Four minutes.

As he neared the main stairs, Molly's quiet crying tore at his heart. He just wanted to get her to a place where she never had to cry again. To get Belisario out of their lives for good.

Liam would be ringing the doorbell soon and Derek wanted to be in place to do the most damage while they had the element of surprise. The two men talking allowed him to slip down the stairs without anyone hearing him.

He eased himself around the corner and kept to the wall, taking small steps toward the kitchen.

Three minutes.

"So Ms. Humphries, Mr. Waterman didn't think he'd

be here for thirty minutes. And it looks like we're coming up on the ten minute mark. What do you think, your other pinky this time?"

Derek expected Molly to cry more at that, but after a moment of quiet she spoke.

"You know what, Belisario, go—"

Derek couldn't clearly hear the rest of Molly's statement, but he was pretty sure that what she wanted Belisario to do to himself was anatomically impossible. Derek smiled at her spunk. That was his girl.

"We'll see if you're so spirited in two minutes," Belisario replied.

Derek felt the silent vibration in his pocket. A text from Liam.

At least three minutes out. Not going to make it in time.

Damn it. Molly didn't have three minutes.

Forget the doorbell. Derek texted him back. Get here as soon as you can and come in loud and hot.

K. Stay away from the front door.

Derek put his phone back in his pocket and eased to the corner, dropping low so he could peek around without being spotted. He only needed one second to ascertain the situation.

Belisario stood across from Molly; one of his men stood directly behind her. Brandon Han, alive but restrained, was on the other side of the table, injured.

If he had to do this alone, he would round the corner, take out the guard closest to Molly, then Belisario. He damn well wasn't going to sit here while another finger was broken.

Derek was about to make his move when he felt the muzzle of a gun against the back of his head.

Damn it.

"Stand up. Keep your hands up, too." The man took

Derek's weapon out of his hand and nudged him forward with his gun. They rounded the corner.

"Boss."

"Ah, Mr. Waterman," Belisario said. "It seems like you were able to join us just a little sooner than you thought."

"I like to be early for my parties." Derek made eye contact with Molly, giving her a half smile, hoping it would be encouraging. She was pale and visibly sweating.

"And where is the other person who was supposed to be with you? Niam, is it?"

"Liam. He'll be here soon."

"Not soon enough to save Ms. Humphries from another broken bone, I'm afraid."

Derek watched as Molly blanched, the last of the color draining from her face.

"How about if you break one of mine instead, if you've got some weird fetish with the bone-breaking thing." It wouldn't be the first bone he'd ever had broken. Growing up on a ranch in Wyoming had made sure of that.

And it would be much less painful than watching Molly suffer more.

Which evidently Belisario had figured out. "Oh, no," he said. "I'll keep my word. One of Ms. Humphries bones every ten minutes."

Derek dove for the other man, he didn't care if it got him shot. But Belisario's two goons grabbed him before he could pound the man's face in like he wanted to. One on each arm, they dragged him back.

Brandon leapt across the table at Belisario when he came near Molly again, but Belisario clocked him in the head with the butt of his gun. Han fell unconscious to the floor.

Molly backed away from Belisario as he came closer to her, fear obvious on her face.

"Stop, or I shoot your boyfriend in the kneecaps, then still break your finger."

Molly stopped. Belisario took a step forward.

Then the whole front of the building seemed to cave in with a huge crashing noise.

Liam had arrived.

Derek took advantage of the men's confusion and yanked himself from their grips. He hit the first one with an uppercut that no doubt broke the man's nose and sent him straight to the floor. Derek leapt behind Molly's couch, landing hard on the floor, knowing Belisario's other man would be shooting at him. Bullets flew past him, as he grabbed his backup weapon from his ankle holster. He felt a searing pain in his arm as a bullet grazed him.

Scrambling to the side, Derek jumped up from the side of the couch the man wasn't expecting. Derek was able to get off a shot before the man could turn his gun back toward him. He fell dead from Derek's chest shot.

Derek rushed over to Molly, putting her directly behind him as Liam wrestled with Belisario. Derek had his weapon raised and Belisario in his sights. He could take the shot and finish Belisario right here. Rid the world of a scumbag.

He had done it many other times with much less reason than he had right now. Judge, jury, executioner.

But he thought of Molly, could feel her hand tucked inside the waistband of his jeans again like she had in the jungle. She trusted him to do the right thing.

"Belisario, put your hands up right now, or so help me God, I will shoot you."

Belisario stopped fighting Liam. He turned and looked at Derek with such a look of malevolence that Derek was sure he was making a mistake by letting the man live. He would have to spend the rest of his life protecting Molly from this possible threat. It would never go away.

But Derek realized he was okay with that. If it meant proving to her—hell, proving to *himself*—that he wasn't the man he used to be, then it was worth it.

Derek lowered his weapon and brought Molly around to his side, careful not to jar her broken finger, as Liam began reading Belisario his rights. Liam was getting his handcuffs out when the henchman Derek had knocked unconscious began waking up and moaned on the ground. Liam's attention was divided for just a moment as he looked over at the man.

Belisario took advantage of it.

He shoved Liam away and grabbed for the gun on the table next to him. He swung it up straight toward Molly.

Derek didn't hesitate. He put three bullets through Belisario's chest. The man died with the same look of evil intent that he'd had when he'd lived.

Derek didn't regret the kill. Not for a split second. The man he had been, the man he was now and the man he would be in the future would always be willing to do whatever he had to do to keep Molly safe.

No matter what.

Chapter Twenty-Five

"You're a moron, you know." Molly rolled her eyes at Derek.

Derek just sat in the chair across from her hospital bed, holding the gauze against his arm where the bullet had grazed him. After their arrival at the emergency room, Molly had insisted that Derek be treated first. She wasn't a medical doctor, but she knew that his bleeding wound needed more immediate care than her broken pinky. Her finger wouldn't get any worse, unlike what his loss of blood could become.

But he'd refused to let any doctors see him until her finger was taken care of.

So now they were waiting for the numbing to take place in Molly's finger so the doctor could reset it. He said it was a clean break, would just need a splint. No permanent damage. Derek's wound, after a quick glance, had also been deemed of the impermanent kind, although it would still need bandaging.

"I'm glad you killed him."

Derek shrugged. "Once he pointed that gun at you he was a dead man."

Molly reached her uninjured hand out to him and he took it. "I'm sorry you had to do it, though. I don't want the taking of another life weighing on you."

"You know, before he pointed the gun at you, when

he and Liam were fighting, I could've taken the shot. It would've been a clean shot, Liam was far enough out of the way. And I thought about it. After everything that had happened, nobody at Omega would've questioned it."

She ran her fingers over his. "Why didn't you?"

Derek stood up and came to stand in front of her where she sat on the hospital bed. He linked their fingers together so that their palms were against each other. "I realized that what you said yesterday was true. The man I was—the decisions I made in the past—they don't define who I am now. I lived in a dark world. But I don't have to stay there anymore."

Molly brought their joined hands to her lips and kissed his fingers. "Well, I'm glad that I never have to worry about him or any of his goons being inside my apartment ever again. So thank you."

The doctor came in and reset Molly's finger, a painless process due to the anesthesia. Not long after, Derek's wound was cleaned and properly bandaged. After the paperwork, they were deemed clear to leave.

"I don't have a house to go home to now," Molly said as they walked out of the hospital in a much less clandestine fashion as when they had snuck out just forty-eight hours ago.

"Yeah, I told Liam to come in loud and hot, but I was envisioning him breaking through the door himself with some uniformed cops, not tearing down your entire dining room with his car."

"I guess I need to check into a hotel or something." Molly hadn't really gotten that far in her thinking. Now that the danger had passed and she wasn't in pain, Molly was bone-weary exhausted.

"How about you let me do something I should've done

after our night together three years ago? Hell, before our night together three years ago."

"What's that?"

"Move you in with me. Court you. Win your heart. Not necessarily in that order."

Molly smiled up at him as he turned her around and leaned her against the car. "You've already done one of those things. A long time ago. The other two, I think, can be arranged."

Derek looked down at her in the way she had always dreamed of having him look at her. "You're the strongest person I know, Molly. I love you."

He kissed her.

"But you're still in trouble for locking me in the clean room."

Molly wrapped her arms around his neck. "I love you, too. And maybe I can find a way to make it up to you."

"Yes. But after you rest. You need some sleep." He trailed a finger down her cheek.

"Okay, but it involves me wearing a lab coat and heels." She got in the car as he opened the door for her. "And nothing else."

She saw his eyes bug out and his whole body jerk. She smiled wickedly back up at him. He made her feel wicked and sexy and smart and strong.

He leaned down and kissed her, taking her breath away. "Okay, maybe sleep can wait."

* * * * *

Look for more books in Janie Crouch's
OMEGA SECTOR: CRITICAL RESPONSE
miniseries in 2016.
You'll find them wherever Harlequin Intrigue books and ebooks are sold!

#1617 SCENE OF THE CRIME: WHO KILLED SHELLY SINCLAIR?
by Carla Cassidy

Sheriff Olivia Bradford's assigned to clean up corruption in Lost Lagoon. The last person she expects as deputy sheriff is Daniel Carson, a man she'd shared a night with five years before—her daughter's father...

#1618 BLUE RIDGE RICOCHET
The Gates: Most Wanted • by Paula Graves

Undercover agent Nicki Jamison and a wanted FBI staffer, Dallas Cole, must work together to bring down a dangerous militia group. When Nicki is abducted, Dallas will do anything to be reunited with her and her irresistible charm.

#1619 BULLETPROOF BADGE
Texas Rangers: Elite Troop • by Angi Morgan

Undercover Texas Ranger Garrison Travis vows to protect witness Kenderly Tyler from Mafia assassins while clearing himself of murder charges. On the run, they find more than adrenaline pulsing between them, but can they actually make it out alive?

#1620 FULLY COMMITTED
Omega Sector: Critical Response • by Janie Crouch

Agent Jon Hatton's best chance to catch a serial rapist is forensic artist Sherry Mitchell. Jon knows Sherry's determined to help catch this criminal, but keeping her safe is his priority. Followed by making her his bride.

#1621 COLORADO WILDFIRE • by Cassie Miles

Presumed dead, Wade Calloway has returned to the only person who can help him take down a dangerous cartel, Sheriff Samantha Calloway—his wife. If they can finish his assignment, they just might find a fresh start.

#1622 SUSPECT WITNESS • by Ryshia Kennie

A witness to murder, Erin Argon threatens a biker gang's deadly secret. She flees to foreign shores, where CIA agent Josh Sedovich finds her, but can he alone keep her safe?

REQUEST YOUR FREE BOOKS!
2 FREE NOVELS PLUS 2 FREE GIFTS!

H HARLEQUIN®

INTRIGUE

BREATHTAKING ROMANTIC SUSPENSE

YES! Please send me 2 FREE Harlequin® Intrigue novels and my 2 FREE gifts (gifts are worth about $10). After receiving them, if I don't wish to receive any more books, I can return the shipping statement marked "cancel." If I don't cancel, I will receive 6 brand-new novels every month and be billed just $4.74 per book in the U.S. or $5.49 per book in Canada. That's a savings of at least 12% off the cover price! It's quite a bargain! Shipping and handling is just 50¢ per book in the U.S. and 75¢ per book in Canada.* I understand that accepting the 2 free books and gifts places me under no obligation to buy anything. I can always return a shipment and cancel at any time. Even if I never buy another book, the two free books and gifts are mine to keep forever.

182/382 HDN GH3D

Name	(PLEASE PRINT)

Address		Apt. #

City	State/Prov.	Zip/Postal Code

Signature (if under 18, a parent or guardian must sign)

Mail to the **Reader Service:**
IN U.S.A.: P.O. Box 1867, Buffalo, NY 14240-1867
IN CANADA: P.O. Box 609, Fort Erie, Ontario L2A 5X3
**Are you a subscriber to Harlequin® Intrigue books
and want to receive the larger-print edition?
Call 1-800-873-8635 or visit www.ReaderService.com.**

* Terms and prices subject to change without notice. Prices do not include applicable taxes. Sales tax applicable in N.Y. Canadian residents will be charged applicable taxes. Offer not valid in Quebec. This offer is limited to one order per household. Not valid for current subscribers to Harlequin Intrigue books. All orders subject to credit approval. Credit or debit balances in a customer's account(s) may be offset by any other outstanding balance owed by or to the customer. Please allow 4 to 6 weeks for delivery. Offer available while quantities last.

Your Privacy—The Reader Service is committed to protecting your privacy. Our Privacy Policy is available online at www.ReaderService.com or upon request from the Reader Service.

We make a portion of our mailing list available to reputable third parties that offer products we believe may interest you. If you prefer that we not exchange your name with third parties, or if you wish to clarify or modify your communication preferences, please visit us at www.ReaderService.com/consumerchoice or write to us at Reader Service Preference Service, P.O. Box 9062, Buffalo, NY 14240-9062. Include your complete name and address.

HI15

I N T R I G U E

*When she practically runs over a missing man with
a suspicious reputation on a dark mountain road, an
undercover agent must decide if she can trust he's as
innocent as he claims.*

Read on for a sneak preview of
BLUE RIDGE RICOCHET, the second book in
Paula Graves's *heartstopping trilogy*
THE GATES: MOST WANTED.

He didn't know how to deal with someone who didn't
seem to want—or need—one damn thing from him.
Especially after the ordeal of the past few weeks. He
didn't know how to relax anymore, how to sit quietly and
eat a bowl of soup without waiting for the next blow, the
next trick.

He knew his name was Dallas Logan Cole. He was
thirty-three years old and had spent the first eighteen years
of his life in Kentucky coal country, trying like hell to get
out before he was stuck there for the rest of his sorry life.
He was a good artist and an ever better designer, and he'd
spent the bulk of his college years trying to leave the last
vestiges of his mountain upbringing behind so he could
start a whole new life.

And here he was, back in the hills, running for his life
again. How the hell had he let this happen?

"I guess those are the only clothes you have?"

He looked down at his grimy shirt and jeans. They
weren't the clothes he'd been wearing when a group of

men in pickup trucks had run his car off the road a few miles north of Ruckersville, Virginia. The wreck had left him a little woozy and helpless to fight the four burly mountain men who'd hauled him into one of the trucks and driven him into the hills. They'd stripped him out of his suit and made him dress in the middle of the woods in the frigid cold while they watched with hawk-sharp eyes for any sign of rebellion.

Rebellion, he'd later learned, was the quickest way to earn a little extra pain.

"It's all I have," he said, swallowing enough humiliating memories to last a lifetime. "Don't suppose you have anything my size?"

Her lips quirked again, triggering a pair of dimples in her cheeks. "Not on purpose. I can wash those for you, though."

"I'd appreciate that." He was finally warm, he realized with some surprise. Not a shiver in sight. He'd begun to wonder if he'd ever feel truly warm again.

She picked up his empty bowl and took it to the sink. "The bathroom's down the hall to the right. Leave your clothes in the hall and I'll put them on to wash."

"And then what?"

She turned as if surprised by the question. "And then we go to bed."

Don't miss
BLUE RIDGE RICOCHET by Paula Graves,
available February 2016 wherever
Harlequin® Intrigue books and ebooks are sold.

www.Harlequin.com

HIEXP0116

Turn your love of reading into rewards you'll love with
Harlequin My Rewards

**Join for FREE today at
www.HarlequinMyRewards.com**

Earn **FREE BOOKS** of your choice.

Experience **EXCLUSIVE OFFERS** and contests.

Enjoy **BOOK RECOMMENDATIONS**
selected just for you.

PLUS! Sign up now
and get **500** points
right away!

MYR16R

Love the Harlequin book
you just read?

Your opinion matters.

Review this book on your favorite
book site, review site, blog or your own
social media properties and share
your opinion with other readers!

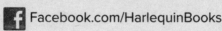
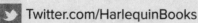

THE WORLD IS BETTER WITH

Romance

Harlequin has everything from contemporary, passionate and heartwarming to suspenseful and inspirational stories.

Whatever your mood, we have a romance just for you!

Connect with us to find your next great read, special offers and more.

f /HarlequinBooks

🐦 @HarlequinBooks

www.HarlequinBlog.com

www.Harlequin.com/Newsletters

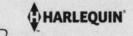

⬙ HARLEQUIN®

A *Romance* FOR EVERY MOOD™

www.Harlequin.com

SERIESHALOAD2015